Spink's
CATALOGUE OF BRITISH
COMMEMORATIVE
MEDALS
1558 to the present day
with valuations

Spink's
CATALOGUE OF BRITISH COMMEMORATIVE MEDALS
1558 to the present day
with valuations

Daniel Fearon

Webb & Bower
EXETER, ENGLAND

For Karen

And that even the *Ladys* may not be defrauded
of the Honor due to the Favourers of this Noble Diversion . . .
John Evelyn, *Numismata*, 1697.

First published in Great Britain 1984 by
Webb & Bower (Publishers) Limited
9 Colleton Crescent, Exeter, Devon EX2 4BY
in association with Limelight Limited
15 Castle Street, Exeter

British Library Cataloguing in Publication Data
Fearon, Daniel
  Spink's catalogue of British commemorative
  medals.
  1. Medals, British—Collectors and collecting
  I. Title
  737°.222°0941   CJ6106
ISBN 0-86350-029-3

Typeset in Great Britain by Keyspools Limited
Golborne, Warrington WA3 3QA

Printed and bound in Spain by Grijelmo Spa

Contents

Acknowledgements

I have had the great advantage over the years of being in contact with so many friendly collectors, dealers and museum staff that it is impossible to say where the information learnt from them has been absorbed into the book. To the collector who struggled with the first typed copy, my especial thanks, both for his corrections and suggestions, and for the loan of a number of medals for illustration. From the seashores of our own South coast to the seashores of New Zealand, and from many places between, the help and advice has been most welcome. Patrick Finn has given me continuous and much needed encouragement. Douglas Liddell, as Managing Director of Spink and Son, has ultimately been responsible for seeing that the book was published; however, his enthusiasm for commemorative medals helped me long before this, when, as a young collector, I first went to Spink's in the late 1950s. The help of Mark Jones has made the viewing of the British Museum collection a pleasant task, and likewise Graham Pollard has allowed me to handle some of the wonderful rarities in the Fitzwilliam Museum.

A large number of the illustrations used are from direct photographs; many were taken by Peter Davey, and originally used to illustrate our *Spink Coin Auctions* catalogues, and also *The Numismatic Circular*. Robert Carson cleared with the Trustees of the British Museum the use of certain illustrations, which were taken directly from the plates of *Medallic Illustrations*. Messrs. Sotheby Parke Bernet & Co. London also supplied a number of original photographs. The white metal medal of Hermit, the Derby winner of 1867, is reproduced by kind permission of the Trustees of the British Museum. The photograph of the Penny Black stamp was kindly supplied by Robson Lowe at Christie's. The final rush to get items photographed has been most expertly handled by Charles Nickols.

My father, Henry Fearon, with his fine command of the English language, and my wife Karen, with her typing skills have both been of immense help in getting all the pieces of the book together. To all who have helped – my sincerest thanks.

Introduction and Background

Historical medals have been struck in this country for many centuries and since the reign of Queen Elizabeth I, that far off and romantic period of our history, have made a lasting and continuous record of events of the times. Visually historical medals resemble coins in that they are usually round pieces of metal stamped or cast with a device on either side, but they have no value as legal tender and their role, whilst initially commemorative, is often artistic as well. The word MEDAL often causes confusion, and today it is, by popular conception, thought of as an item pinned to the chests of the military as a record of service; or should the recipient have been brave enough, as a mark of esteem for a particular act of bravery. The origins of the word are in the latin *metallum* (metal), and it was used in old English to describe coins, awards and commemorative items without any distinction. MEDALLIONS, from the same origins, described larger objects, not necessarily of metal, that would record, in relief, an event or a person: thus plaster decorations on ceilings, and brass insets on furniture, are known by this name. In this book both words will be found, but wherever possible I have restricted myself to the word *medal*. War medals and bravery awards are not of this book: indeed that is another area of numismatics which others far better qualified than I am have already catalogued.*

The modern medal is a product of the Renaissance. It emerged in France with experiments by silversmiths; and it emerged in Germany as an extended form of jewellery, a personal and lasting memento – a method, indeed, of reproducing the traditional painted miniature in a manufactured form. In Italy the medal began as a unique art form. The same reasons were behind its emergence as were found elsewhere, but sponsorship from the wealthy families, each seeking self-preservation, gave rise to an art not fully practised since Roman times. The great Lords gave each other expensive gifts, and more often than not, a medal as well – a medal that would flatter the donor with a kind but correct portrait, and a suitable legend. The English were not pioneers of early commemorative medals, and at the period where this book commences (with the accession of Elizabeth I to the Throne) the country was as insular as it had ever been, and European ideas were not being adopted. Only three years earlier the Spanish head of Philip II had been placed on coins of the realm, and it was only a few years earlier still that the strong religious links with the Church in Rome, once fostered by Henry VIII, had been abruptly severed. There was to be exactly thirty years before the Spanish Armada attempted to invade our shores. So with good reason, by the time the medal became firmly established in this country, it had changed from being an often large cast bronze masterpiece to a more modest, more easily manufactured talisman, recording the events, sometimes strictly factually, sometimes with comment, and often in both these cases, with satire in the comment.

With the English Civil War, the changing political state added the new concept of the medal as a badge of allegiance and, sometimes, as a military reward. The Glorious Restoration of Charles II in 1660 saw the introduction of the large struck silver medal, a Dutch concept, pioneered here by the medallist John Roettier. The more personal, small, neat style of Thomas Simon, so suited to the Commonwealth, was overtaken, and with good result. It is an interesting fact that the medallists in the employment of

---

*JOSLIN, E. C. Spink's Catalogue of British and Associated Orders, Decorations and Medals, with valuations. *A complete revised handbook edition, 1983. 192 pages, 290 × 170 mm (11¼″ × 6¾″), 350 illustrations including 70 in colour, 1750 valuations, ribbon colour chart, and index. Published by Webb and Bower.*

The Royal Mint (as it is now known), were permitted to use the Mint machinery, out of hours for their own benefit. Thus whilst most of the important English medals, from the 17th to mid-19th century were actually struck at the Mint, there are virtually no records, for all the transactions were private commissions to the medallist. This was as true with the works of the great Wyon family of medallists in Victorian times as it was when Samuel Pepys – recording yet another sideline of the Mint medallists – wrote down in his Diary on March 26th, 1666: '. . . to the Tower, to see the famous engraver (John Roettier), to get him to grave a seal for the office'. Control at the Mint was strict, but as the history of our coinage shows, records appertaining to the actual numbers of coins struck have always been subject to much guesswork, and the mystery created by this almost total lack of records with medals makes the collecting of them take on a new depth. It is not so much the danger of sailing into uncharted waters, as the pure pleasure of finding out for oneself just as many details as possible.

The history of the medal progressed with the emotive anti-Papal issues of the late Charles II and James II period, erupting with the triumph of the Protestant Restoration of William and Mary, with many medals, like the Royalty commemorated on them, imported from Holland. The early 18th century was dominated by the wars in Europe, which saw the historical victories commemorated rapidly in the readily available form of the medal, albeit as some would point out, with a certain sameness to many of them. The Royal Society for the Promotion of Arts and Commerce tried to revive this trend with medals for the victories of George II and George III in the 1750s and 1760s. It was, however, with the birth of modern industry and the vision of one great manufacturer, Matthew Boulton, that the cheap medal was developed, first with a strict eye kept on the quality of the design and the finished product (often much discussed with a pompous correspondence), but changing rapidly when the imitators moved in, to the production of the cheap souvenir item. And thus it remained, very much unchanged, right up to the outbreak of war in 1914.

With the ending of hostilities the worried world had little time for the inconsequentials, and in modern times that is sadly what medals have become. Another war, and more recently inflation, has seen the incentive of the medallist and issuer of medals virtually destroyed. There is always an aura of splendour about the Past, and to some collectors our modern commemorative medals may well seem dull and mediocre. Such is progress! Probably the collectors of a hundred years ago, examining the huge output of truly terrible medals struck for Queen Victoria's two Jubilees, felt that there was little or no future for them! New generations develop new tastes and a new curiosity, and it can be safely said that there will always be collectors of British Historical Medals. And if this book gives encouragement, then so much the better, for that is its purpose.

The Manufacture of Medals

There have always been two entirely separate ways of manufacturing medals, by casting and by striking. The earliest modern medals, those of the Renaissance period, were mostly cast productions. First the artist would model the subject in wax, usually mounted on a glass or slate background, and from this a mould would be made. From the mould the medals would be cast. In recent years the cost of die-sinking has become so high that many artists are reverting their ideas back to the cast medal. Today new methods allow for freer style and the whole medal can be cast in a quick and easy process. The collector of cast medals looks for sharpness of detail: for example the medallist may have used a pair of dividers to etch two fine circles that would contain, between them, the letters of the legend. In good early casts these lines often can be seen. Casting can be easily abused, for once the original model had been destroyed or broken (it didn't take long in the early days) then the next generation of casts would have to be made from a surviving medal, and so on, with after-casts made from after-casts, and the definition and quality becoming poorer at each stage.

To strike a medal, in the years before mechanisation, the design would be cut directly into the soft steel die. The image would be the opposite to the intended finished item, and for the high relief the deeper the medallist would have to cut. For lettering and some of the other features the medallist would use a series of prepared punches, which he would have before him, much as a printer would have his type. An untidy box of punches is usually blamed for simple errors, such as an inverted A – V – for a V, but it was a muddled mind that would invert letters, an Ͷ for an N, obviously confused by working in reverse. As the medallist worked he would make soft metal 'squeezes' so

The original steel dies
used to strike the medal
for the death of Princess Charlotte in 1817,
by T. Webb and G. Mills. (268.6)

that he could see his work in a positive form, and when he was satisfied with it, the die would be 'hardened' and ready for use. Traditionally, the obverse, or front-side die is the bottom one in the press, and this remains static. The lighter reverse die moves with the machinery, to strike a medal with each downward blow.

By the start of the 19th century the French had perfected the reducing machine, making the whole medal-making process much simpler. The artist no longer had to be a specialist in engraving, for he could produce a much larger than life positive model in a soft material, such as plaster. A hard positive impression is then made, for the reducing machine to run a fine point over the design in ever-increasing circles, whilst its other end cuts a similar, but smaller impression into a soft steel die. The dies are hand finished, the lettering added and then 'hardened' to make them ready for striking.

In commerce medal dies are seldom offered for sale. The Royal Mint and private manufacturers usually keep their old dies, but they are bulky objects and hard to store for easy access and reference. The British Museum has a large collection of early medal dies, including many Roettier family ones dating from the 17th century. Alas, steel rusts quickly, and many were impaired long before they came into the Museum's possession. This, and the unsolvable problem of a severe lack of space, prevents them from being displayed. Sometimes an artist's original drawn medal designs are offered for sale. The diarist John Evelyn held the candle for Samuel Cooper, who was drawing a study of the King to be used for the new coinage of 1662, 'he choosing the night and candlelight for the better finding out the shadows'. Later the Camera Lucida and other optical devices would be used to transfer sculptured profiles on to paper for copying.

The dies, drawings, papers and related items all give an added dimension to the collecting of medals. They are all hard items to price, but so seldom seen on the market, that they should be bought whenever possible, as each piece would be a unique addition to any collection.

Leslie Durbin's original plaster model
for the Silver Jubilee medal of Her Majesty the Queen, in 1977.
For the actual medal, issued by Spink & Son,
it was reduced to a diameter of 57 mm. (428.2)

What to Collect and Where to Start

Today's world is one of instant news and comment. A century ago the news was also amazingly instant, with newspapers printing many editions, with a working telegraph system, and with a postal service that thrived on the efficient results of a low paid workforce. But a century ago this speed was still new and exciting and the purpose of the medal as a record of a newsworthy event was only just changing. It is the newsworthy aspect of the medal that has been its prime use from the beginning of the period covered by this book, and it is through just this aspect that collectors become immersed in history. John Evelyn, the diarist, was also the author of the first book published in the English language which covered the subject of historical medals, *Numismata*, published in 1697; and in it he refers to the medals as 'vocal monuments'. Two better words could not be found. Medals that record an historical event are monuments, small perhaps, but as a lasting reminder they are no lesser thing than the marble plaque or statue, the traditional form of monument. And vocal too, for they speak volumes about people by providing contemporary portraits. They have satire and comment and some simply provide us with a commentary on events both great and small. History, by definition, looks at an event in restrospect, but the medal provided a contemporary comment. With great battles the mood of the victors is exploited, the monarchy praised and the enemy damned. The medal has more permanence than books, paintings or broadsheets, and being small enough to be handed from person to person – for discussion and admiration – it had a good propaganda value as well.

To see some of the rarest medals one must look in museums where they are safely kept for us and for future generations; but what of the lesser medals? The collector will soon find that a great many facets of history can be gleaned from them, and he can learn much by actually holding them in his hands. I find it no bad thing that with some people there is a strong desire to be possessive. Present day collectors are fed by the dispersal of a previous generation's collecting. Objects, not only medals, pass from hand to hand and are kept and admired and in due time passed on. There is not the sterile perfection of a museum display. There is true excitement in hunting down certain pieces and true pleasure in owning them.

I have always found medals such personal things that it is hard to give advice as to what to collect. This book is not intended for those who buy a medal today for £100 in the hope that tomorrow it will be worth £200. True collecting comes from the heart and not the wallet. It is sensible to try to pick a theme, and in this book there are many that can be pursued: Battles, Ships, Planes, Portraits and Personages, the works of one artist, Political or Economic History, Trains and Transport, and so on. The list is a long one. Contain your collecting habits! A good small collection is always more attractive than a large unmotivated and messy accumulation. Age is not everything. For some the first commercial flight of Concorde is as great an event as the circumnavigation of the globe by Sir Francis Drake. Mass production increases scope and the Victorian era provides the collector with a wonderful supply of material commemorating the most far ranging events.

A general rule with any form of collecting is always to try to buy the best. Torn paintings and books with pages missing are not accepted; and so it is with medals, but with one important difference – many pieces were issued as souvenirs or pocket pieces and with these one's own sense of judgement will soon tell which are the ones best forgotten! Some collectors enjoy buying medals with a history of good ownership behind them, 'Ex Montagu, Murdoch, Bute or Northumberland', the background giving a sense of security and authenticity. To buy the best, it is best to buy from the best! All the established coin dealers also handle the sale of historical medals, and usually carry a stock that starts at only a pound or so an item. There are now several individual dealers who specialise in the subject. The beginner is advised to buy from a dealer he trusts and the recently formed British Numismatic Trade Association has many members all over the country who will always be helpful. My own Company, Spink and Son, keeps its stock of historical medals in a splendid, large old cabinet that has been used since the turn of the century. Our advice is free and friendly for, of course, it is to our benefit to encourage new collectors! We publish *The Numismatic Circular* ten times each year, and historical medals are listed in most editions. The standard of cataloguing and editorial comment in the Circular is high without being overbearing; well worthy of its status as the longest continuously published numismatic journal offering items for sale. It started publication in December 1892. Spink is also the only British dealer running major auctions throughout the year and some of these include specialist sections devoted to historical medals. The beginner is advised to be a little wary of auctions, for the items offered tend to be expensive and the buyers professional, whereas the dealer has an item in stock offered at a fixed price with no uncertainty about it. There is time for discussion and not the snap decision needed to make an extra bid. Most dealers will offer advice on pieces being offered for sale at auctions and will then for a modest commission (usually 5%), bid for the collector. To me this has always seemed to be the best value – the collector gets good and cheap advice and the dealer bids for him not against him, and is happy to be seen making the purchase. Both the major auction houses, Sotheby's and Christie's hold regular coin and medal sales, but other than Spink Coin Auctions, Glendining and Co. is the only company whose sales are devoted entirely to coins and medals. There is now a regular 'Coin' press with periodicals and annual publications and these carry advertisements for the leading dealers. It has often been said that the bigger the dealer the bigger the stock, and the bigger the stock the cheaper the prices; and there is much truth in this. Look around, see what is available, but always try to buy the best. A rare medal in poor condition will in fifty years probably be considered a little rarer, but it will still be in the same poor condition, whereas quality will always shine through. But be prepared to bend the rules, for medals are very much visual objects and the decision to buy is therefore a personal one. The attraction is what the medal looks like or means to you; not the fact that it has been graded as 'extremely fine condition' by some leading authority.

Legends and Dates

On many medals the legends are found in Latin; originally this was so because the medal was made to have instant international appeal, and Latin was the single common language to the whole of Europe. From those early days it soon developed into a tradition. For those unfamiliar with Latin names and dates a brief summary is given. One further confusion is the use of the letter V for U, thus:

CHARLES—CAROLUS—CAROLVS

Other monarchs' names are:

ELIZABETH—ELISABETHA or ELISAB.
JAMES—IACOBUS
WILLIAM—GUILIELMUS or GUIL.
MARY—MARIA
ANNE—ANNA
GEORGE—GEORGIUS
VICTORIA—VICTORIA
EDWARD—EDWARDUS

The legend following the monarchs' names usually continue (though often in an abbreviated form) – DEI GRATIA ANGLIA, FRANCIA ET HIBERNIA REX/REGINA – BY THE GRACE OF GOD KING/QUEEN OF ENGLAND, FRANCE AND IRELAND.

For the dates the Latin numbering is also often used:

M — 1000
D — 500
C — 100
L —   50
X —   10
V —   5
I —   1

The numerals are combined to make up the date by adding numbers together, VI for 6 or III for 3, but some numbers are shown as being less than the next nearest figure, thus IV for 4, IX for 9 and XC for 90. This book commences at the date 1558 which would be shown as MDLVIII, and, for a final example, the year of Queen Victoria's accession – 1837 – is MDCCCXXXVII. Some medals adopt a form of dating that creates quite a puzzle, for certain letters in the legend are larger than others; the large letters are picked to form the date. The small medal for the Gunpowder Plot in 1605 is an example. The chronogrammatic legend reads, NONDORMITASTI ANTISTES IACOBI (Thou, the keeper of James, hast not slept); the larger letters when rearranged make MDCIIIII – 1605.

Display and Storage

In an ideal situation a collector would wish to sit surrounded by his possessions, each piece easily available, so should some visitor come by, he, too, could share the pleasure of it. Traditionally, coins and medals are kept in wooden cabinets specially made for the purpose, but today there is only one maker left in England producing high quality cabinets. These cabinets usually have a single bank of twenty thin trays behind double locking doors, and are a little more than a cubic foot in size. Each of the trays has shallow round holes in rows, different sizes in different trays and these take the coins or medals. Each of the holes has a felt roundel in the bottom to prevent scratching, and there is a small piercing at the bottom of each of these holes so that by holding the tray one can push the medal out from below. In this way there are no broken fingernails – which was obviously a problem in 1697 – for Evelyn writes with much enthusiasm of the collector who placed a small ribbon under each piece, so that 'One easily raises up the medal ... without pinching or digging it forth with one's nails, which is inconvenient, and often sullies it'. These holes also can accommodate a collector's ticket, a roundel of card on which the details of the medal are recorded – a system which, says Evelyn in his next sentence 'being extremely neat and ready, I recommend for others imitation'. A good new cabinet will cost some £300, the price of an expensive medal or two, and if it can be afforded is a worthwhile investment. Old cabinets do appear in auction sales, but invariably they are in need of repair – or having been purpose-made to house a specific collection, the trays contain an assortment of

*A modern cabinet by H. S. Swann, made of mahogany with a rosewood trim
to the trays, especially adapted for medals with deeper trays
in the bottom section. The trays have a variety of different sized holes
and there is a small hole at the bottom of each so that the medal in the tray can
be eased out by pushing from underneath with a finger.
A reprint of* Medallic Illustrations *is open on top of the cabinet.*

irritating and odd-sized holes. The serious collector should consider forsaking a couple of medals for the sake of a good cabinet that will suit his own collecting needs. There are German and Italian companies producing well made plastic cabinets, sometimes housed in carrying cases, which have trays of regular square holes. These are cheaper, lighter, and in the short term just as serviceable. Some medals are so decorative that it is a pity to have them locked away unseen and a table-top glazed display case is then the best answer. Alas, these are as hard to find as many of the medals, and a diligent search of antique shops and sale rooms is required.

Some collections are forced by the pressures of the world we live in to spend more and more time locked away in boxes and bank vaults or in similar secure homes. In these cases place the medals in paper – not plastic envelopes. Paper 'breathes', but a sweaty thumb print on a medal being placed in a plastic envelope creates enough moisture to ruin pieces in most metals. An old-fashioned cellophane envelope will help protect a proof-like surface, and this as well as 'breathing' has the advantage of being transparent.

A set of the Diamond Jubilee medals of Queen Victoria, 1897,
issued by Spink and Son, showing the portrait bust by Frank Bowcher
and a selection of reverse types. (348.3)

Sometimes a wall display is suitable, with medals pinned to the background of a deep frame, often with additional material for added interest. Even now medals can be found with original advertising sheets dating back two hundred years or so. Medals of buildings can be shown with old prints or drawings of the same date. In some cases old sale invoices, showing the selfsame medal selling in the dim-distant past for a fraction of its present-day value, give a new dimension. The obvious drawback, of course, is that most medals are two-sided and once mounted one side is lost to the viewer. Spink and Son will always advise customers on cabinets or displays. Unlike coins, some medals are extremely large, and many of these come in elaborately designed fitted cases, worth preserving, but which, alas, will never fit into any ordinary cabinet. Spink also provides a service to customers whereby collections can be kept in our own security vault. A modest charge is made for this service, based on the value of the collection, thus really only making it worthwhile for those of some importance.

Security and Good Records

The theft of collections is a reality which has to be faced. As a dealer, the writer is not only very much aware of it, but is deeply concerned by its steady, continuing growth. In the course of a single year, the list of works of art, though not necessarily numismatic items stolen is, indeed, a long one. Other than to emphasise the constant need for security, the actual details of this thieving are outside the general scope of my book. However, where I propose to advise is in the preparation of a proper catalogue of the whole collection. The placing of tickets underneath each of the pieces has already been mentioned, but this is obviously of no use should they be stolen along with the collection! An added precaution is necessary! More work for the collector! Yet here may I stress that it is a pleasant kind of work! Let us look first at the formation of the proposed catalogue. A card index or a loose-leaf file may well be the best method for a

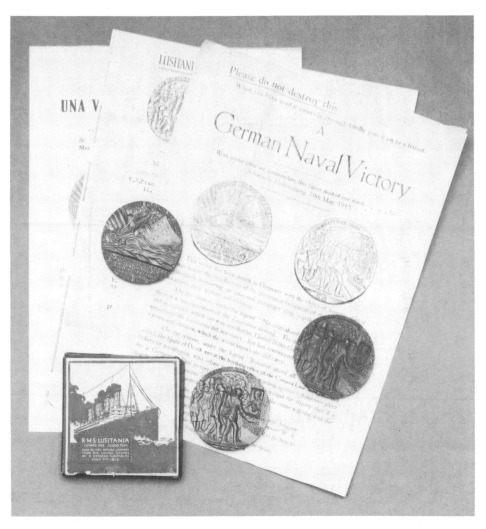

The Lusitania medals with the original box of issue and the splendid
propaganda leaflet that went with it. The medals were sold for 1s. each.
The Red Cross and St. Dunstan's were the two main beneficiaries. (366.3)

growing collection, for then each new medal, as it is acquired, can be written up and
inserted into its correct order, date by date. The loose-leaf file has the advantage of
being more portable, though it is a curious thing that however much one writes down
about a medal, collectors develop a most retentive memory for all the items that they
own. This is a good thing!

The catalogue should record *all* details relating to the medal: the subject, the date,
the medallist, and details of the design and legend being essential. The cost, place of
purchase, pedigree (if known), references to similar medals in published catalogues
should be recorded, and perhaps also the track record of similar medals being offered
for sale in dealers' lists or auction catalogues. This last being information that can
continually be brought up to date. Historical details about the medals and the
background to their being issued can also be mentioned. It takes a little self discipline
to settle into the most suitable style, but building up these details are just as much a part
of collecting as the hunt for the medal itself. *Keep the records away from the collection
itself*, so that in the event of a theft they can be made readily available to the police. The
police are greatly concerned with the theft of works of art, coins and medals and the
like and have a well established Fine Art Squad, but the numismatic trade has
developed a magnificent 'early warning' system and by using the telephone and telex
messages, details of stolen property are known to all the major dealers around the
world, with a particular emphasis on the dealers in this country. Speed is of an essence,
and it works, for several important collections have already been located and recovered
because of the system.

Good insurance cover, like the security, is outside the scope of the book, but it
should be pointed out that most general household policies do not cover coins and

medals and, therefore, extra cover is required. On valuable collections many insurance companies will also insist on a professional valuation, and this is another area where Spink can help. Insurance companies like good records (though they do not reduce the premiums because of them) and records can be improved by good black and white photographs of all the pieces in the collection. The professional photographer will go to great lengths to explain the difficulties in producing good results, and the amateur will probably find him right! However, photography is itself a rewarding hobby and to be able to link it with collecting is a most useful asset.

Grading

Coin collectors and dealers have used a standard of grading that has become universally accepted. The system is simple and also works, and is indeed used, for the grading of historical medals. In addition to the terms described below there are the useful adjectives 'about' or 'nearly', which are sometimes used to indicate that the medal is perhaps generally better than a fixed grade, but not quite as good as the next grade. Edge knocks, discoloration, corrosion, dents and scratches are also noted in addition to the grade. Some pieces are found pierced and sometimes the piercings are plugged – all this would be added to the basic grade. A toned medal should be so described, the implication being that the tone improves the piece, unless it is otherwise stated. The actual grades are:

F. – FINE
The medal would show noticeable signs of wear over the entire surface, fine details such as hair, might be entirely worn away from high spots.

V.F. – VERY FINE
The wear on the medal would be limited to the high spots, the remaining details would all be clear. The pieces would be quite pleasing to look at – and certainly acceptable to a collector.

E.F. – EXTREMELY FINE
The medal in this grade has been handled, but shows no really obvious signs of wear. There may be a few minor hairline scratches, but it would seem to be more or less as it was when it was made.

F.D.C. – FLEUR DE COIN
This is reserved for items that are in truly perfect mint state with their original bloom or lustre (fleur), and devoid of any flaws. Coins in this condition are also described as 'uncirculated' but medals were never intended for circulation, so, for medals, this grade is only used in ignorance.

PROOF
A proof is a trial or special striking of a medal for which a general or ordinary issue then follows. The term is *NOT* a grade. Because so many proof coins are made with 'brilliant' surfaces the term has been used to describe medals with similar surfaces. Again, this is not correct.

The Cleaning of Medals

The long accepted rule about cleaning has always been 'Don't!' Old advice is often the best but there will always be cases where some cleaning is necessary. Modern medals are now often issued with a brilliant 'proof-like' surface. These sometimes discolour and should you be unfortunate to get one that does, I suggest that it is left well alone. Older medals have usually seen some handling and are therefore easier to deal with. Never *polish* a medal: there is a world of difference between cleaning and polishing, for the latter very soon rubs off all the fine details and highlights. A little detergent (the washing-up kind) with a drop of water gets rid of the dirt of ages. On silver medals only methylated spirits will also do this, at the same time leaving a pleasant blue tinge. Silver that has turned black with age can be left for a while in household cloudy ammonia which should, once the colour has shifted, be washed off. Dry the medal with the softest of cloths as tough material will scratch. A medal cleaned in ammonia will have no tone. I hesitate to suggest that a tone should always be added but sometimes it improves the look of a medal. So place the medal in a saucer of Domestos and it will very soon turn an 'antique' grey colour – remove it at once and rinse it well. Old copper medals which have some wear on them can be given a pleasant look or finish by a gentle brushing with a soft cloth – a very soft shoe-shine brush will do or one of those old-fashioned curved, narrow brushes for cleaning silver. Sometimes a touch of natural (not silicone) furniture polish, applied and brushed off, will give a new life to an old and dull copper medal. Gold will clean gently in lemon juice and will not be harmed by a quick dip in Silver Dip, though *never* clean silver medals in this. If you have the urge to clean some of your medals, first buy a cheap one that can be used to practice on and if ever there is any doubt in your mind leave the medal alone until you are able to discuss it with a professional. This paragraph is not intended to give the impression that many or most medals need a thorough cleaning the moment you get them home. Silver pieces develop a wonderful tone over the centuries that should never be touched, gold acquires a red hue, copper and bronze lose their brilliance and white metal dulls with age. Treat all your medals with the greatest of care and remember that cleaning is the removal of dirt. In all times of doubt, follow the rule of the first sentence above and *don't* clean the medal.

Some additional words may be added here simply as a caution when actually handling medals. Medals are always best handled by the edge or rim. A heavy thumb print right in the centre of a brilliant silver medal will probably stay with it forever. Even worn medals deserve handling with some respect for their age, for only one careless slip is needed to make a severe edge knock or a deep scratch. The 'brilliant' mirror surface first appears on medals at the end of the 18th century, the brilliance of 200 years should be preserved. Other medals, such as the Royalist Badges of Charles I, were made for wearing and are now found with the defects one might expect, but mishandling today can ruin the natural smoothness that might have come from (one would like to think) a Caroline leather jerkin. Always hold medals over a table with a soft covering – even careful people sometimes drop them, and when showing medals to friends, warn them too, to be careful. The traditional medals were made to be handled, all those centuries ago. Don't be afraid to handle them now, but be cautious and careful, and you will be preserving them for other generations to enjoy.

Clubs, Societies and Museums

Most collectors wish to share their knowledge with others and there are a number of numismatic clubs and societies up and down the country. The coin periodicals publish future events and talks and *The Numismatic Circular* has always made a regular feature of local society news. The British Numismatic Society is the senior society which directs its resources to British numismatics, whereas The Royal Numismatic Society has, overall, much wider margins. A collector of historical medals may feel that these societies devote too much of their time to coins, but societies can only reflect the interest of their members and membership should be encouraged at all levels.

Guides to national and local museums are published each year and are worth studying to find out the museums which house Numismatic Collections. Many of the local museums display all the pieces that are of a specific local interest, and so many of these pieces are unfortunately outside the range covered by this book. Their interest, however, is enormous. The National Collection is housed in the British Museum where there is a small permanent display. Most pieces remain in the safety of the Department of Coins and Medals and a student ticket will get you access. The collection belongs to us all, do not be afraid to go along and see some of the pieces in it. In Glasgow, the Hunterian Museum Coin Cabinet recently commemorated the 200th anniversary of the death of the founder of the collection, William Hunter, by opening a new Coin Gallery, where there is a permanent display. This lively and purpose made exhibition – the only one in the United Kingdom – brings to life the subject of numismatics. Its importance to medal collectors is that is is a 'closed' collection, for nothing was added after the death of its founder. This means that all the medals in the collection can be guaranteed to be at least 200 years old, and that no 19th Century fantasies or restitutions have crept in to confuse us today. The display includes a working 'Mint' where commemorative souvenir medals are hand struck in the manner of medieval coins. There are fine collections in the Museum of Birmingham, Belfast, Dublin and Edinburgh, while the collections of the Ashmolean Museum in Oxford and the Fitzwilliam Museum in Cambridge come under the educational umbrella of the universities. Museum staff are extremely helpful and informative, and are happy to spend time with collectors. I have always been grateful to a Deputy Keeper at the British Museum who devoted much of a wet Saturday morning to the questions put to him by a thirteen-year-old schoolboy and whose enthusiasm pointed me to an eventual career in professional numismatics.

Pleasure and Investment

These two words have been linked with all kinds of numismatic collecting for some two decades, as a direct result of the various promotions for the 'alternative investment'. It seems that today fewer and fewer good items are available costing under £10, but do not be put off by my use of the word 'good' or the arbitrary figure. There are many, many medals which can still be purchased for under £10, and although they may not be perfect or artistic or of a precious metal, they tell the same story, have the same background and are just as 'newsworthy' to a collector as the grander items. These are the medals collected for pure pleasure, the pieces one buys simply because one likes them. The more expensive the medal becomes, the more considerations there are to be taken into account before the actual buying of it, and one of the most important of these is the question of value. Is the medal worth the price being asked for it? What will the medal be worth in a few years time? Coins and medals are things which cannot be charted in a Financial Times index, though this publication of mine will now provide the first guide in the commemorative medal series. Investment in some shares can be very much for the short term, the quick turnover and sale at a profit, whilst others are bought for their stable price and steady yield. And so again with medals, though in a much less drastic way. A 'booming' economy creates a market, those who bought before it all started sell at a profit, new buyers move in and then, too, sell at a profit, whilst those who bought at the peak must wonder at the wiseness of their investment. But this is really not the name of the game, for the alternative investment of medals must be seen over the long term; certainly I would suggest a five year period, preferably ten years or more. This way the erratic movement caused by outside influences will have been more than evened out, leaving a good steady climb. Collecting, by nature of the very word, means a continual adding to the pieces one already has; thus a single medal of Elizabeth I may be rare and after a period of some ten years be worth a sizeable premium, but during those ten years the collector will have added further medals of Elizabeth I to his single piece. The comfort and security of numbers – now a *collection* of the medals of Elizabeth I – this is where the value lies. The value of the first single piece is all but forgotten when the total value of all the pieces is assessed and compared with the total expenditure. In the market one medal of Elizabeth I will attract one or two keen collectors, but a group of fifty pieces would be of *great* importance and would attract a far greater number of potential buyers, thus generating a widespread interest.

It is always a good thing to rely on instinct, to make the odd mistakes and learn from them, but whilst you will be collecting medals that have a special personal appeal, you should always be aware of the financial ties, for in these difficult times the need for money is never far away. In the past, good individual medals have proved to be excellent investments, and collections of medals have fared even better. So long as you never let yourself forget the 'Pleasure' of collecting the 'Investment' will look after itself.

The Form of this Book

The form, order and background originated in a most wonderful book, published almost one hundred years ago, *Medallic Illustrations of the History of Great Britain and Ireland to the Death of George II*, compiled by Edward Hawkins and edited for publication after his death by Augustus Franks and Herbert Grueber*. The book published by the British Museum and based on the main European museum collections, as they stood at that time, lists thousands of items in its two volumes, and it is a most thorough and complete record, though ending at 1760. *My* book has taken the items of Royal and National historical importance and placed them in a simple

---

*HAWKINS, E. Medallic Illustrations of the History of Great Britain and Ireland to the Death of George II. Edited by Sir A. W. Franks and H. A. Grueber (1885). Reprinted 1977. In two volumes. 725 and 866 pages; woodcuts. Cloth.
The plates to the above. Reprinted in one volume. 1980. 183 plates with descriptive text. Cloth.

chronology. Thus date by date the events that made our history, and are recorded with medals, are now listed. And by way of continuity, a few events for which no medals are known are also listed. The entries are arranged in date order by title, by artist (where known), by size and by metal; and sometimes a few comments concerning the pieces are added. Wherever possible a valuation figure appears with each description. Each entry is numbered in sequence year by year and entries prior to 1760 carry a reference to the relevant entry in *Medallic Illustrations*. For the period 1760–1837 reference is made to the recently published *British Historical Medals**, the first volume of Laurence Brown's worthy continuation. My system of numbering enables the book to be used readily as a simple 'Dictionary of Dates' or 'Calendar of Events'. For some of the major events ten or more medals may be known, but in these cases I have had to select the items which are the most available as, after all, my book is primarily designed as a guide for collectors. Where possible, I have listed medals of English manufacture, but where no such medals exist, yet foreign-made medals do, then these are listed. Some private and personal medals have been omitted, not because they are not worthy of listing, but because they do not have a place in a simple chronology, and likewise some of the many anniversary medals are missing for exactly the same general reasons. I have tried to concentrate on those items a collector might be able to buy and although valuations are given I would emphasise that the book is by implication (and sub-title) only a guide.

The Descriptions and Valuations

The description of each medal begins with a reference numeral in the left-hand column. The changing dates of the events form a separate column to the left of the descriptions. The date is the date shown on the medal, the date of the event being commemorated – a comment that is not as obvious as it might at first seem. Most medals are struck shortly after the event through some are known to have been issued within days. Others, like Coronation medals, are issued in anticipation of the event (hence the large number of Edward VIII pieces). There was nothing unusual, either, in John Kirk's medal for 'The Conquest of Canada' being struck three years after the event, in 1763. There is not nearly enough room in this type of a general catalogue to give the full details of the images on the medals, so the descriptions tend to be not much more than a title. Where a description of the design of the reverse (back) is given, it is preceded by the symbol, ℞. The name of the medallist is given where known, and every description gives the diameter in millimetres and the name of the metal in which the medal is most usually found, abbreviated to the traditional N – gold, R – silver, $Æ$ – copper or bronze, Pt – platinum, Pb – lead, Al – Aluminium, WM – white metal or tin and Fe – Iron. The final column is reserved for valuations, about which I now add a word of caution. The figures that appear are not the digestions of a large computer that has been fed all the latest information from price lists and auction sale results. They have been arrived at simply as a result of having first studied the subject as a collector, and then for twenty-one years as a professional, working firstly for Sotheby's in London and New York and, since 1971, as part of the team that makes up the Coin Department at Spink and Son. Some may argue that such a method is, if nothing else, a little haphazard, but it has stood me well over the years – and it also underlines that the emphasis of this book is to be a guide. Values are not given for the rarest items and as the book lacks space to designate rarity, the valuation is used as a form of compensation. The figures, also, try to reflect market availability. *All the prices quoted are intended to reflect the price that the specialised dealer might reasonably ask of a collector, and the price assumes the medal to be a pleasing example in 'very fine' or better condition.* It is worth considering just how rare some of the medals are. For instance, in the series of Coronation medals an issue of 1,000 specimens is considered common. Shouldn't one think, therefore, that the official 1661 Coronation medal of Charles II would be worth much more than a Gothic Crown of Queen Victoria issued in 1849? Yet 8,000 specimens of this Crown were struck, and at a price of £600 or more (which it now fetches) it is more than three times the price of the Coronation medal. I would stress that my valuation figures are there to encourage collectors into the market. Established coin collectors will have to adjust their views on grading, rarity and values and start collecting medals for the pleasure of owning items connected with the making of our history. It is my hope that all readers will now find for themselves that it is a pleasure indeed to buy, purely to satisfy one's own collecting instincts.

* *BROWN, L.* A Catalogue of British Historical Medals 1760–1960. *Volume I. The accession of George III to the death of William IV. 1980. 469 pages; illustrations. Index, appendixes. Cloth.*

Further Reading and Reference

Books are an essential part of medal collecting and provide information and understanding. Full and detailed bibliographies are published but the following titles (to which I have added some comments), are offered for sale by Spink & Son and are listed in their free annual catalogue, 'About those Coins'.

> HAWKINS, E. Medallic Illustrations of the History of Great Britain and Ireland to the death of George II. Edited by Sir A. W. Franks and H. A. Grueber. 1885, reprinted 1977. Two volumes.

The essential reference up to 1760, with a particularly good introductory essay on the subject of medals. Earlier, in writing about 'The Form of the Book', I explained how *Medallic Illustrations* has provided the essence of this book. It was a monumental task completed almost a century ago, though for the continuation we look to another splendid book that has only just been published. This is . . .

> BROWN, L. British Historical Medals, 1760–1960. Volume 1, 1760–1837, published 1980. (Two further volumes to follow.)

This first volume covers the events up to the death of William IV and again there is a good introductory essay. The text is well defined and filled with a wealth of historical notes and there are a great number of photographic illustrations of a well selected number of medals. It is expensive, but when the final two volumes are published it will be an irreplaceable guide for the historical student, *and* the collector, to learn more about the subject of medals.

> WHITING, J. R. S. Commemorative Medals, a medallic history of Britain from Tudor times to the present day. 1972.

Perhaps the best of the more recent general guide books, with many well thought out ideas on the subject.

> LINECAR, H. W. A. The Commemorative Medal, its Appreciation and Collection. 1974.

Another well written and comprehensive guide book by a most respected authority.

> WENT, A. E. J. Irish Coins and Medals. 1978.

Very much a guide, but containing a lot of information on Irish medals that is not easily found elsewhere.

The original drawing of John Rennie, by his nephew George, that was copied by the medallist W. Bain for the medal struck on the opening of the Sheerness Docks in 1823. It is interesting to note that in the medal the direction has been reversed and the bust faces to the left. (274.4)

WOLLASTON, H. British Official Medals for Coronations and Jubilees. 1978.

The only guide to this popular series of medals.

FORRER, L. Biographical Dictionary of Medallists, B.C. 500–A.D. 1900. 8 volumes. Upwards of 5,000 pages. 1904–1930. Reprinted.

Another monumental work and the accepted source of information on the artists and engravers of medals and coins.

JONES, M. The Art of the Medal. 1979.

The book written for the superb exhibition at the British Museum and organised by the author, who has also published three other useful booklets on medals:

– The Dance of Death, medallic art of the First World War. 1979.
– Medals of the Sun King. 1979.
– Medals of the French Revolution. 1977.

The Art of the Medal contains some original and well described observations on English medals.

HILL, Sir G. F. Medals of the Renaissance. Revised and enlarged by Graham Pollard. 1978.

The essay on early English medals is useful and concise, and one of the supplementary plates concentrates on English medals. Hill's, now hard to find, *Guide to the Exhibition of Historical Medals in the British Museum* (1924) probably still remains the best general introductory guide to the subject of English medals.

The best of the more recently published introductions to numismatics – coins and medals, ancient and modern, is:

GRIERSON, P. Numismatics. Soft and hard covers. 1979.

Auction catalogues are often used as references in all the many varied fields of numismatics and with commemorative medals many of these catalogues provide information not found elsewhere. In particular the collector of English medals will soon become familiar with the catalogues of the collections formed by H. Montagu (Sotheby, 1897), H. Murdoch (Sotheby, 1904) and H. Farquhar (Glendining, 1955). More recently Spink Coin Auctions No. 8 (February, 1980) was a composite catalogue with an excellent range of English medals covering the period 1588–1885.

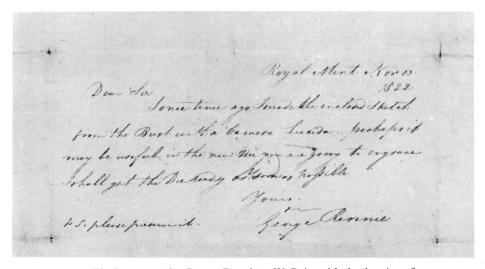

The Letter sent by George Rennie to W. Bain, with the drawing of
his uncle, John Rennie. It is dated November 13, 1822.
George Rennie was employed at the Royal Mint; the bust he refers to
was by the sculptor Francis Chantrey, and is
now preserved in the National Portrait Gallery.

The Medal, faithful to its charge of fame,
Through climes and ages bears each form and name
In one short view subjected to our eye,
Gods, Emperors, Heroes, Sages, Beauties lie.
                                    Alexander Pope.

HOUSE OF TUDOR

Elizabeth I
(17 November 1558–24 March 1603)
Born 7 September 1533, daughter of Henry VIII
and Anne Boleyn; half-sister of Queen Mary
(1516–1553–1558)

Medals had established themselves as part of the European heritage during the century preceding the accession of Elizabeth I, but England was slow to follow, in spite of some obvious missed opportunities. The French celebrated the expulsion of the English in 1455 with a medal that was a triumph of the medieval engraver's art and the style was nowhere copied. The Coronation of Edward VI, in 1547, saw the first medal issued in this country commemorating such an event, but for Elizabeth there was no medal. Most of the medals of her reign are small pieces often no more than jettons, often of Dutch origin. There are exceptions and the Naval Reward Badge of 1588, by Nicholas Hilliard, is a brilliant example. Portraiture is rare on Elizabethan medals, but here Hilliard pioneered a medal that was really a three-dimensional form of the miniature painted portrait, and a form that could be produced in small numbers, each the same, for special presentation purposes.

Date	No.			Pic.	MI	Metal	Value
1558	1.1	*Accession*. Phoenix medallet,	29 mm	*	3	Æ	250
	1.2	*Mary Queen of Scots*. Marriage to Francis (later Francis II), 30 mm		*	4	Ꞃ	—
		● In 1832 J. B. Salmson made a larger copy (52 mm) of this counter, which was struck in gold, silver and copper at the Paris mint.					
		Church of England. Re-established. *No medal.*					
1559	2.1.	*Francis II*. As King of Scotland,	28 mm		9–11	Ꞃ Æ	450 150
		Coronation. No medal					
1560	3.1	*The Peace of Edinburgh*. Francis and Mary,	32 mm		18–20	Æ	150
		● France recognises Elizabeth as Queen.					
	3.2	*Francis II*. Death, French medal,	53 mm		21	Æ	400
		● Modern French mint restrikes exist.					
	3.3	*The New English Coinage*. Counter,	29 mm	*	22–23	Æ	150
		William Shakespeare. Birth. *No medal*					
		● A great number of medals exist relating to Shakespeare, often being issued for anniversaries, etc.					
1565	8.1	*Mary, Queen of Scots*. Marriage to Henry, Lord Darnley, 41 mm		*	43–44	Ꞃ	—

* The asterisk in the 'Pic.' column indicates that the medal is illustrated.

Date	No.		Pic.	MI	Metal	Value
1567		*Murder of Darnley. No medal.*				
1572	15.1	*Elizabeth, Recovery from Smallpox.* By J. Primavera, 61 mm	*	49	Ꝃ	—
	15.2	*Defence of the Kingdom.* Medallet, 25 mm	*	57	Ꝃ	150
1574	17.1	*Elizabeth.* Phoenix Badge, 44 mm		70	Ꝃ	—
1579	22.1	*Mary, Queen of Scots.* Personal counters 28 mm	*	77–82	Ꝃ	125
1580	23.1	*Sir Francis Drake.* Voyage around the World (1577–1580), medal with engraved map, by M. Mercator, 69 mm	*	83	Ꝃ	—
1585/6	28.1	*Assistance to the United Provinces (Holland).* Counters, 30 mm	*	86–87	Ꝃ	100
1587	30.1	*Mary, Queen of Scots.* Beheaded. 19th C. medal, by J. Tassie, 55 mm		98	Æ	150
	30.2	*Protestants Supported in Belgium.* Dutch medal, 53 mm	*	99	Ꝃ	400
	30.3	*Leicester Quits Belgium.* (usually later restitutions), 48 mm	*	100–102	Ꝃ	150
1588	31.1	*Defeat of the Spanish Armada.* Counter, 32 mm	*	113	Ꝃ	125
	31.2	*Defeat of the Spanish Armada.* Dutch medal (Pope and Kings), 51 mm	*	111	Ꝃ	400
	31.3	*Defeat of the Spanish Armada.* Dutch medal (Church on rock), 51 mm		112	Ꝃ	500
	31.4	*Defeat of the Spanish Armada.* Naval Reward (Ark on waves), 51 × 29 mm	*	119	Ꝃ	—
1589	32.1	*Elizabeth, 'The Dangers Averted'.* Personal award, by Nicholas Hilliard, 48 × 44 mm	*	129	A̶/ Ꝃ	— —
1590	33.1	*James VI, of Scotland.* (later James I of England), marriage of Anne of Denmark, 41 mm	*	137	A̶/	—
1596	39.1	*Alliance of England, France and United Provinces.* Dutch medal, 52 mm	*	140	Ꝃ	400
	39.2	*Alliance of England, France and United Provinces.* Counters, 29 mm		141–146	Ꝃ	80
	39.3	*Invasion Defeated.* Dutch medal, 51 mm	*	148–150	Ꝃ	800
1597	40.1	*Spanish Defeats in the Netherlands.* Dutch medal, 51 mm		152	Ꝃ	400
	40.2	*Spanish Defeats in the Netherlands.* Counters, 30 mm		153–156	Ꝃ	80
1600	43.1	*Battle of Nieuport.* (800 English killed or wounded), Dutch medal, 52 mm	*	171	Ꝃ	500
1601	44.1	*Distress Relieved.* Possibly a pattern coin, 26 mm	*	177	Ꝃ	350
		Robert Devereux, Earl of Essex. Executed for Treason. *No medal*				
1603		*Elizabeth.* Death. *No contemporary medal.*				

HOUSE OF STUART

James I
(24 March 1603–27 March 1625)
Born 19 June 1566, son of Mary, Queen of
Scots and Henry, Lord Darnley; great-great
grandson of Henry VII

During the reign of James the medals issued, though often small in size, became more English in style, though not necessarily in manufacture. The reign produced a number of medals of private people and also the splendid engraved medals by Simon de Passe. The Coronation medal was the first *official* medal to be struck in England to commemorate (and be distributed at) the event.

Date	No.		Pic.	MI	Metal	Value
1603	46.1	*Coronation.* The first official medal for an English Coronation, 29 mm	*	11	Æ	300
	46.2	*Queen Anne.* Coronation. Portrait and companion to previous, 29 mm	*	12	Æ	350
1604	47.1	*Peace with Spain.* Portrait medal often found with open work scrolled border, 38 mm	*	14	Æ	200
1605	48.1	*The Gunpowder Plot.* Dutch counter, 29 mm	*	19	Æ Æ	125 40
1609	52.1	*Alliance of England, France and the United Provinces.* Dutch medal, shields joined by cord, 53 mm		22	Æ	400
	52.2	*Alliance of England, France and the United Provinces.* A similar Dutch counter, 32 mm		23	Æ Æ	80 40
	52.3	*Alliance of England, France and the United Provinces.* Dutch medal, three hearts. 53 mm	*	25	Æ	400
1610		*Prince Henry, Created Prince of Wales. No medal.*				
1611		*'Authorised' version of the Bible published. No medal.*				
1612	55.1	*Henry, Prince of Wales.* Death. By C. Anthony (?), 29 mm	*	29–31	Æ	250
1613	56.1	*Princess Elizabeth* (Daughter of James I). Marriage to Frederick, Count Palatinate, 38 × 29 mm	*	32	Æ	800
1615	58.1	*Maurice, Prince of Orange.* Created a Knight of the Garter, 55 × 46 mm		39	Æ Æ	650 150
	58.2	*Lady Arabella Stuart.* Death in the Tower. 19th century medal, 51 mm		41	Æ	65

Date	No.		Pic.	MI	Metal	Value
1616	59.1	*James I; Queen Anne; Charles, Prince of Wales.* Engraved portrait medals by S. de Passe, 56 × 43 mm	*	61–67	Æ	850
	59.2	*Prince Charles.* Matriculation at Oxford University, 19 mm	*	71	A/ Æ	1000 550
		Death of Shakespeare. No contemporary medals. (See 1560)				
1618		*Sir Walter Raleigh executed. No medal.*				
1619	62.1	*Queen Anne.* Death, 44 mm		75	Æ	—
	62.2	*The Synod of Dort* (Dortrecht). Dutch medal, Council assembled, ℞ rock, 58 mm	*	77	Æ	400
	62.3	*The Synod of Dort* (Dortrecht). Dutch medal, Belgic lion, ℞ arms,	*	79	Æ	400
	62.4	*Charles, Prince of Wales.* Cliché, 23 mm	*	81	Æ	80
		● A cliché is a uniface medal struck on a thin flan, thus making the reverse side a simple indentation of the obverse.				
1620		*Pilgrim Fathers sail for North America. No medal.*				
1625		*James I.* Death. *No contemporary medal.*				

Charles I
(27 March 1625–30 January 1649)
Born 19 November 1600, second and only surviving son of James I

The early medals of the reign show the French influence of the work of Nicholas Briot, but the Civil War was to establish two great English medallists, Thomas Rawlins and Thomas Simon. The development of the medal as a badge of loyalty or reward firmly established itself during this reign. The continued use of the small counter-sized medal is found, and indeed, it was much used during the reign.

Date	No.		Pic.	MI	Metal	Value
1625	68.1	*Marriage to Henrietta Maria.* Small double-portrait jetton, 22 mm	*	1–2	Æ	20
1626	69.1	*Coronation.* Official medal, by N. Briot, 30 mm	*	10	Æ	250
	69.2	*Coronation.* Portrait cliché, by N. Briot, 25 mm		11	Æ	60
1627	70.1	*Attack on the Isle of Rhé.* French medal of Louis XIII on Buckingham's defeat, 44 mm	*	20	Æ	150
1628	71.1	*Tribute to Henrietta Maria.* Counters, 28 mm	*	23–24	Æ	40
	71.2	*Expedition to La Rochelle.* Possibly a pattern Halfcrown, 36 mm		32	Æ	—
1629	72.1	*Order of the Garter Augmented.* Counter, by N. Briot, 22 mm	*	33	Æ	100
1630	73.1	*Birth of Prince Charles.* Counters, 30 mm	*	34–36	Æ	40
	73.2	*Baptism of Prince Charles.* Counters, by N. Briot, 30 mm		38–39	Æ	40
	73.3	*Dominion of the Sea.* Large cast portrait medal, by N. Briot, 58 mm		40–41	Æ	1200

Date	No.		Pic.	MI	Metal	Value
	73.4	*Dominion of the Sea.* Small counter, by N. Briot, 28 mm	*	42–43	Æ	80
1632	75.1	*Cecil Calvert, second Lord Baltimore and Anne, Lady Baltimore.* Granted Maryland, portrait medal, 44 mm	*	52	Æ	—
1633	76.1	*Coronation in Scotland.* Official medal, by N. Briot, 28 mm	*	59–61	Æ	120
	76.2	*Return to London.* By N. Briot, King mounted, ℞ City view, *Usually cast* 43 mm	*	62	Æ	120
	76.3	*Birth of Prince James.* Counters, 30 mm		64–65	Æ	50
1635	78.1	*Three Children of Charles I.* Small medal, by N. Briot, after Van Dyke painting, 32 mm	*	72–74	Aᵥ Æ	1500 250
1636	79.1	*Dutch Fishery Treaty.* Portrait medals of Charles I and Henrietta Maria, by Hans Reinhard, 76 mm	*	81–84	Æ	—
1637	80.1	*Bishop Juxon, Lord Treasurer of England.* Counter, 27 mm	*	85	Æ	120
		● Juxon was present at the execution of Charles I and was given a pattern 5-Broad piece by the King. This unique gold coin is often called the 'Juxon Medal' and is now in the British Museum.				
1638	81.1	*Prince Charles, Installation as Knight of the Garter.* Portrait medal, 27 mm	*	87	Æ	150
	81.2	*Prince Charles, Installation as Knight of the Garter.* Non-portrait, by N. Briot, 30 mm	*	88	Æ	75
1639	82.1	*The Scottish Rebellion.* King on horseback, by T. Simon, 32 mm	*	90–94	Æ	150
	82.2	*Destruction of Dutch Fleet off Dover.* Dutch medal, 63 mm		95–96	Æ	—
	82.3	*Dominion of the Sea.* Similar portrait medal to 73.3, by N. Briot, 60 mm	*	97	Æ	1200
1640	83.1	*Charles I.* Complimentary counter, 28 mm		99	Æ	—
1641	84.1	*Princess Mary.* (Daughter of Charles I) marriage to William of Orange. By J. Blum, 72 mm	*	100	Æ	600
	84.2	*Princess Mary.* Marriage medal, by S. Dadler, 63 mm		101	Æ	500
	84.3	*Thomas Wentworth, Earl of Stafford.* Beheaded, by T. Simon, 25 mm		102	Aᵥ	—
1642	85.1	*Declaration of Parliament.* Oval badge, by T. Rawlins, 46 × 37 mm		108–109	Æ	400
	85.2	*Robert Devereux, Earl of Essex.* Oval badge, with border, 44 × 37 mm (Also found without border.)	*	113	Æ	300
	85.3	*Battle of Edgehill.* Military reward, by T. Rawlins, 38 × 30 mm	*	119	Æ	1500
1643	86.1	*'The Forlorn Hope'.* Military reward, by T. Rawlins, 42 × 33 mm		122	Æ	—
	86.2	*Ferdinand, 2nd Lord Fairfax.* Military reward, portrait badge, 38 × 27 mm		126	Æ	600
	86.3	*Bristol Taken.* Medal with city view, by T. Rawlins, 29 mm		131	Æ	
	86.4	*Peace or War.* Struck after Royalist victory at Bristol, by N. Briot, 28 mm	*	134–136	Æ Æ	90 35

Date	No.		Pic.	MI	Metal	Value
	86.5	*Edward Montagu, Earl of Manchester.* Military reward, portrait badge, 32 × 27 mm		137	Æ	350
	86.6	*Prince Charles.* Portrait badge, by T. Rawlins, ℞ Arms (? 1643), 49 × 34 mm	*	263	Æ	1000
1644	87.1	*Sir Richard Brown.* Military reward, portrait badge, 34 × 28 mm	*	142	Æ	350
		Battle of Marston Moor. No medal.				
1645	88.1	*William Laud, Archbishop of Canterbury.* Executed, by J. Roettier (struck *c.* 1660s), 58 mm	*	147	Æ	350
	88.2	*Sir Thomas Fairfax.* Military reward, portrait badge, by T. Simon, 35 × 30 mm	*	150	Æ	250
		● A smaller version of this badge, 24 × 20 mm, was also issued.				
	88.3	*Prince Rupert, Count Palatine.* Military reward, portrait badge, by T. Rawlins, 38 × 30 mm	*	159	Æ	1500
		Battle of Naseby. No medal.				
1645		*Cromwell.* Lt-General of the New Model Army. *No medal.*				
1646	89.1	*Earl of Essex.* Death, by T. Simon 20 × 18 mm	*	165	A/	1500
					Æ	350
1647		*Charles I.* Imprisonment at Carisbrooke Castle, I.O.W. *No medal.*				
1648	91.1	*Giles Strangways.* Release from the Tower, by J. Roettier (struck *c.* 1660s), 60 mm	*	177	Æ	350
	91.2	*Call to Unanimity.* By N. Briot (similar to 86.4), 28 mm		179–181	Æ	150
1649	92.1	*Charles I, Execution.* By T. Rawlins, ℞ anvil, 42 mm		187	Æ	300
	92.2	*Charles I, Execution.* By T. Rawlins, ℞ Salamander, 42 mm	*	188	Æ	300
	92.3	*Charles I, Execution.* By T. Rawlins, ℞ rock, 29 mm	*	190	Æ	100
	92.4	*Memorial Badge.* Several varieties of small badges		194	Æ	150
	92.5	*Memorial Medal.* By J. Roettier (struck *c.* 1660s), 51 mm	*	200	Æ	50
	92.6	*Memorial Medal.* Similar, but smaller 34 mm		201	Æ	100
	92.7	*Memorial Medal.* Issued by Oxford University, 29 × 33 mm		205	Æ	200
	92.8	*Memorial Medal.* German (?) medal, signed F ℞ seven headed monster, 47 mm	*	210	Æ	250

Throughout the period of the Civil War badges were issued by friends and partisans of the Monarch. Those badges which are specifically rewards, and some badges of the military leaders (of both sides) are listed in the date sequence. Many are the work of Thomas Rawlins and some are signed. The badges were intended for wearing, some have scrolled or leafed borders, others even have pearl drops suspended from them (representing tears shed for the Royalist cause), and some are found with 'Martyr Populi' or similar inscriptions added after the King's execution. For further reading see M.I. pp. 353–371. Items 93 and 94 below are a summary of types:

	93.1	*Charles I and Henrietta Maria.* Uncrowned, large.	*		Æ	350
	93.2	*Charles I and Henrietta Maria.* Uncrowned, small	*		Æ	150
	94.1	*Charles I and Henrietta Maria.* Crowned, large			Æ	350
	94.2	*Charles I and Henrietta Maria.* Crowned, small			Æ	150
	94.3	*Charles I* (alone). Uncrowned, ℞ incuse arms.			Æ	180
	94.4	*Charles I* (alone). Crowned, ℞ crowned arms.	*		Æ	250

Date	No.		Pic.	MI	Metal	Value
	94.5	*Charles I* (alone). Uncrowned, small.			Ꞧ	150
		● Badges of Prince Charles, issued during the exile, are listed under the reign of Charles II.				

During the reign of James I and Charles I numbers of engraved counters were issued. The sovereigns of England are known in two designs and complete sets, sometimes in silver boxes with Royal portraits, are extremely rare.

	95.1	*Sovereign Counter.* Full length Ꞧ arms,	28 mm			Ꞧ	15
	96.1	*Sovereign Counter.* Half length Ꞧ armorial shield, 28 mm				Ꞧ	30
	97.1	*James I and Prince Charles (I).* Portraits,	29 mm			Ꞧ	30
	98.1	*Charles I and Henrietta Maria.* Portraits,	29 mm	*		Ꞧ	30

THE COMMONWEALTH

Oliver Cromwell
(Lord Protector, 16 December 1653–3 September 1658)
Born 25 April 1599; M.P. for Huntingdon.
His death occurred on the anniversaries of
the Battles of Dunbar and Worcester.

Richard Cromwell
(3 September 1658–resigned 25 May 1659)
Born 4 October 1626, died in exile, 12 July 1712

The Commonwealth period, in spite of its strict Puritanism, was to produce some splendid medals, many by Thomas Simon. The wars with the Dutch saw that they also produced medals for the events of the period. Cromwell himself was not portrayed on many medals, though his 'Lord Protector' medal is often collected along with medals of the Coronation series.

Date	No.		Pic.	MI	Metal	Value
1649	99.1	*John Lilburne's Trial.* (For libelling Cromwell), by T. Simon, 34 mm	*	3	Ꞧ	250
					Æ	65
1650	100.1	*Henry Ireton.* Portrait, by T. Simon, 30 × 29 mm		5	Ꞧ	—
	100.2	*Cromwell, Lord Protector.* Uniface high relief portrait, by T. Simon (oval, and often on round flan). 19th c. strikings, 30 × 28 mm	*		Æ	80
	100.3	*Naval Reward.* By Order of Parliament, by T. Simon, 24 × 22 mm		12	A/ Ꞧ	—
	100.4	*Battle of Dunbar.* Military reward suggested by Cromwell, by T. Simon, bust Ꞧ Parliament, 25 × 22 mm	*	13	A/ Ꞧ	—
	100.5	*Battle of Dunbar.* 18/19th C. uniface striking of obverse	*		Ꞧ	100
					Æ	60
	100.6	*Battle of Dunbar.* Larger, but similar (both sides), 34 × 29 mm		14	Ꞧ	150
1651	101.1	*Charles II, Coronation (at Scone) as King of Scotland.* Last medals, 32 mm	*	18	Ꞧ	500
		● Designed by Sir James Balfour. An unique struck example was sold by Spink Coin Auctions, March 1984.				
		Battle of Worcester. Charles II defeated. *No medal.*				
1652	102.1	*Inigo Jones, Architect.* Death, by J. Kirk. 18th C., 32 mm		25	Æ	80

Date	No.		Pic.	MI	Metal	Value
1653	103.1	*Naval Reward.* Similar to 101.3, but with arms of Scotland, by T. Simon, 56 × 51 mm	*	26–27	A\	—
		46 × 37 mm		28	A\	3500
	103.2	*Admiral Tromp.* Dutch medal, 71 mm		32–33	AR	750
	103.3	*Cromwell, Lord Protector.* By T. Simon, usually contemporary casts, 38 mm	*	45	AR	125
1654	104.1	*Peace with Holland.* Dutch medal, by O. Müller, 80 mm	*	50	AR	1500
1655	105.1	*Subservience of France and Spain.* Dutch medal, 47 mm		60	AR	—
1656	106.1	*Archbishop James Usher (of Dublin).* By W. Mossop Jr., struck 1820, 41 mm		61	WM	75
1657	107.1	*William Harvey, Death.* 19th c. medal, by A. Durand, 41 mm		64	Æ	15
1658	108.1	*Battle of Dunkirk.* French medal, by J. Mauger, 41 mm		70	Æ	25
	108.2	*Cromwell and Massaniello.* Dutch medal, by O. Müller, 73 mm		78	AR	800
		● Tomaso Aniello, called Massaniello, was the leader of a revolt (against tax on fruit) in Naples. This, and the following medal, compares the two leaders.				
	108.3	*Cromwell and Massaniello.* Italian medal, by F. St. Urbain, 50 mm	*	79	AR	400
					Æ	100
	108.4	*Cromwell, Death.* By T. Simon. Contemporary casts also exist, 22 × 19 mm	*	82	AR	150
	108.5	*Cromwell, Death.* Small Dutch copy, 29 mm	*	84	A\	1150
					AR	150
	108.6	*Cromwell, Death.* Large Dutch copy, 48 mm		85	AR	400
1659		*Richard Cromwell, Resignation. No medal.*				

Charles II
(30 January 1649–29 May 1660–6 February 1685)
Born 29 May 1630, eldest son of Charles I

The evidence of the Continental influence absorbed during a ten-year exile is shown by the rapid growth of the use of the medal as a commemorative item, a political item and an item for Royal patronage. John Roettier came to England at the Restoration and was the leading medallist for the rest of the century. Thomas Simon's work was still accepted, in spite of his Commonwealth positions, but his death during the plague of 1665 left the way open for Roettier. The medals of this reign are to be admired for their high technical and artistic standards. Larger and more obviously impressive medals become more common place, and use of the lettered edge is seen on many of them.

During the exile a number of portrait badges of Charles were issued and worn by his supporters. The fashion started with Charles I and continued to cover the Restoration and Marriage of Charles II. Badges then ceased to be a medallic influence, though they appear from time to time – the Diamond Jubilee of Queen Victoria (1897), being such an event in more modern times.

Date	No.		Pic.	MI	Metal	Value
1649–1660	110.1	*The Exile*. Portrait badges,	*	1–31	Æ	85
		● The Exile Badges. These come in three sizes: 18 × 15 mm, 25 × 19 mm and 32 × 28 mm, and all show varieties of portrait busts.				
1660	111.1	*The Restoration*. Portrait badges, 35 × 29 mm	*	39–42	Æ	100
	111.2	*Embarkation at Scheveningen for England.* Dutch medal, by P. van Abeele, 70 mm	*	44	Æ	800
	111.3	*The Landing at Dover*. By J. Roettier, 57 mm	*	48	Æ	1000
	111.4	*The Restoration*, 'Felicitas Britanniae'. A magnificent large medal, by J. Roettier, 84 mm	*	53	Æ	1500
		● The Restoration and the arrival of Charles II in London on his birthday, 29 May, was a widely celebrated event. Only three medals are listed here.				
	111.5	*The Restoration*, 'Britanniae'. By J. Roettier, 62 mm		54	Æ	550
	111.6	*The Restoration*, 'Moses'. By T. Simon.		56	Æ	150
	111.7	*General George Monk, Duke of Albemarle.* Badge. By A. and T. Simon, 37 × 30 mm		65	Æ	500
1661	112.1	*Coronation*. Official medal. By T. Simon.	*	76	A/ Æ	1000 150
	112.2	*Coronation*, 'Dixi Custodian'. By T. Rawlins. ℞ Charles as shepherd, 33 mm		78–82	Æ	400
1662	113.1	*Marriage to Catherine of Braganza* (daughter of John IV, King of Portugal). 'Majestas et Amor'. By G. Bower, 27 mm	*	91–92	Æ	80
	113.2	*'The Golden Medal'*. By J. Roettier. A fine portrait medal with busts either side. Undated, but for the marriage, 43 mm	*	111	Æ	150

● So named in a poem by Edmund Waller.
Our guard upon the royal side!
On the reverse, our beauty's pride!
Here we discern the frown and smile;
The force and glory of our isle.

Date	No.		Pic.	MI	Metal	Value
	113.3	*Queen Catherine, as St. Catherine*. By J. Roettier, 43 mm	*	112–113	Æ	160
	113.4	*Marriage* Portrait badges.	*	96–104	Æ	85
		● The Marriage Badges. These either show portraits of Charles II and Queen Catherine or Catherine alone; there are several varieties, 19 × 15 mm to 30 × 27 mm.				
	113.5	*Dunkirk sold to France*. French medal. By J. Mauger, 41 mm		127	Æ	40
1664		*New Amsterdam re-named New York. No medal.*				
1665	116.1	*Naval Reward* (The Dutch fleet defeated by James, Duke of York, off Lowestoft). By J. Roettier, 56 mm		140–141	Æ	500
	116.2	*Naval Reward, The Duke of York's Medal*. By J. Roettier, 64 mm	*	143	Æ	550
	116.3	*The Dominion of the Sea*. By T. Simon. An exquisite medal, usually struck from damaged reverse dies, 28 mm	*	145	Æ	500
		● Simon is believed to have died of the plague – this is his last known work.				
		The Great Plague of London. No medal (but see item 117.4).				
1666	117.1	*Proposed Commercial Treaty with Spain*. By J. Roettier, 56 mm	*	161–162	Æ	550
	117.2	*Naval Action with Dutch, Admiral de Ruyter*. Dutch medal by O. Müller, 79 mm		167–168	Æ	600
	117.3	*Naval Action with Dutch, Admiral Tromp*. Dutch medal by O. Müller, 80 mm		172	Æ	600
	117.4	*The Fire of London (and the Plague)*. Unique medal in British Museum, 36 mm	*	173	Æ	—
1667	118.1	*Ships Burnt in the Medway, near Chatham*. Dutch medal by P. van Abeele, 72 mm		174	Æ	1500
	118.2	*The Peace Breda and Alliance of England and Holland*. By J. Roettier. ℞ Britannia (modelled by Frances Stuart, Duchess of Richmond), 56 mm	*	185–186	Æ	300
	118.3	*The Peace of Breda and Alliance of England and Holland*. Dutch medal, by C. Adolfzoon. ℞ Dutch and English ships sailing together, 44 mm	*	184	Æ	300
	118.4	*Charles II and Catherine*. Undated portraits, by P. Roettier, 27 mm		192	Æ	150
	118.5	*The State of Britain*. Undated, by P. Roettier. ℞ sleeping lion, 27 mm		193	Æ	150
1668	119.1	*Suspension of Hostilities between France and Spain*. Dutch medal, 46 mm	*	197	Æ	—
1669	120.1	*Charles XI, of Sweden, elected a Knight of the Garter*, 42 mm	*	198–200	Æ	300
1670	121.1	*British Colonisation*. Portraits of Charles II and Catherine, by J. Roettier. ℞ Globe, 41 mm	*	203	Æ	200
		Treaty of Dover with France. No medal.				
1671	122.1	*John George II, of Saxony, elected a Knight of the Garter*. A German medallic Thaler, 48 mm	*	205	Æ	250
	122.2	*Charles XI, of Sweden, installed as a Knight of the Garter*. By J. Roettier, 44 mm	*	206	A/ Æ	1500 200
1672	123.1	*John Maitland, Duke of Lauderdale*. Portrait, by J. Roettier, 62 mm	*	208	Æ	500

Date	No.		Pic.	MI	Metal	Value
	123.2	*Battle of Solebay* (off Southwold). French medal, by J. Mauger, 41 mm		209	Æ	45
	123.3	*Declaration of Liberty and Conscience.* By P. Roettier, 55 mm		214	Æ	500
1673	124.1	*Foundation of Mathematical and Nautical School in Christ's Hospital.* By J. Roettier, 71 mm	*	217	Æ	500
		The Test Act (Catholics excluded from office). *No medal.*				
1674	125.1	*The Peace of London (Treaty of Westminster).* Dutch medal. R dove over sea, 61 mm	*	225	Æ	750
	125.2	*John Milton, Death.* Dassier's medal, struck *c.* 1730s, 42 mm		229	Æ	40
1677	128.1	*William III of Orange (and later England) Marries Princess Mary* (daughter of James, Duke of York, later James II). By N. Chevalier, 42 mm	*	235– 236	Æ	200
1678	129.1	*Peace of Nijmegen between Holland and France.* Dutch medal, 28 mm		244	Æ	150
	129.2	*Sir Edmundbury Godfrey, Murdered.* Several medals of the event that was the prelude to the Popish Plot. By G. Bower, 39 mm	*	247– 251	Æ	150
	129.3	*The Popish Plot.* By G. Bower. Usually cast, 37 mm		252	Æ	150
1680	131.1	*James, Duke of York and Mary of Modena* (married 1673). Portrait medal, by G. Bower, 52 mm	*	255– 256	Æ	750
1681	132.1	*Anthony Ashley Cooper, Earl of Shaftesbury.* Released from the Tower, by G. Bower. R view of London, 41 mm	*	259	Æ	120
	132.2	*Charles II, Sir Samuel Morland's medal.* By J. Roettier, 33 mm		257	Æ	350
1682	133.1	*Named Hamet and Keay Nabee.* Ambassadors of Morocco and Bantam respectively, visit England, by G. Bower, 39 mm	*	260	Æ	450
	133.2	*James Butler, Duke of Ormond and Lord Lieutenant of Ireland.* By G. Bower, 51 mm	*	262	Æ	500
	133.3	*James, Duke of York.* Shipwrecked off the Norfolk coast, by G. Bower, 42 mm		263	Æ	—
1683	134.1	*Isaak Walton, Death.* Medal struck in 1824 by E. Avern, 36 mm		271	Æ	50
		● Walton wrote 'The Complete Angler'				
	134.2	*The Rye House Plot* (attempted assassination of Charles II). By G. Bower, 46 mm	*	274	Æ	500
	134.3	*Princess Anne (daughter of James II) Marries Prince George of Denmark.* By G. Bower, 38 mm		275	Æ	200
	134.4	*Charles II, Presentation Medal.* By J. Roettier. R Royal arms, 53 mm		277	Æ	750
	134.5	*Firmness of Charles II.* Dutch medal, by J. Sorberger. R diamond in flames, 56 mm	*	278	Æ	450
1685	136.1	*Charles II, Death.* By J. Roettier, 39 mm	*	289– 290	Æ	150

James II
(6 February 1685–11 December 1688)
Born 14 October 1633, only surviving brother of
Charles II, died in exile at Versailles,
6 September 1701.

The short reign of James II continued to show the influence on medal production that had originated with the jubilant spirit of the Restoration. The events of the reign were to produce a number of interesting, though not necessarily artistic medals. George Bower had previously used the medal to make 'political' comment on the religious state of the country. Now the Seven Bishops gave him cause to continue.

Date	No.			Pic.	MI	Metal	Value
1685	136.2	*Accession.* Small medallet, by C. Wermuth,	18 mm		4	Æ	150
	136.3	*Coronation.* The official medal, by J. Roettier,	34 mm	*			
		(200 specimens struck)			5–	Ν	1500
		(800 specimens struck)			6	Æ	150
	136.4	*Queen Mary, Coronation.* The official medal, by J. Roettier,	34 mm				
		(100 specimens struck)			7	Ν	2000
		(400 specimens struck)				Æ	125
	136.5	*Opening of the Scottish Parliament* (23 April, Coronation Day). R lion,	48 mm	*	10	Æ	300
	136.6	*The Prudence of James.* By G. Bower,	29 mm		11	Æ	120
	136.7	*James II and Queen Mary.* Portraits, by G. Bower,	29 mm		12–13	Æ	120
	136.8	*James II and Queen Mary.* By G. Bower, conjoined busts. R sun,	52 mm		16	Æ	500
	136.9	*James II, 'Tutamen ab Alto'.* Complimentary medal, by G. Bower,	44 mm	*	18	Æ	350
	136.10	*James, Duke of Monmouth.* Defeated at Sedgemore, by G. Bower,	51 mm	*	23	Æ	600
	136.11	*Monmouth, Beheaded.* By G. Bower. R cypher,	51 mm		25	Æ	600
	136.12	*Monmouth, Beheaded.* By J. Smeltzing. R Head spouts blood,	38 mm		26	Æ	400
	136.13	*Monmouth and the Duke of Argyle, Beheaded.* By R. Arondeaux,	61 mm		27	Æ	500
	136.14	*Military and Naval Reward.* By J. Roettier (varieties showing long and short hair),	63 mm		28–29	Æ	600
1687	138.1	*Spanish Wreck Recovered.* £300,000 salvaged off St. Domingo by Capt. W. Phipps. By G. Bower,	55 mm	*	33	Æ	400
		Variety with clouds in sky,	54 mm			Æ	500
	138.2	*Christopher, Duke of Albermarle.* Governor-General of Jamaica (and sponsor of the Spanish Treasure salvage). By G. Bower,	47 mm		34	Æ	1000
		Declaration of Liberty and Conscience. No medal.					
1688	139.1	*Archbishop Sancroft and Bishops (The Seven Bishops) Imprisoned.* By G. Bower,	51 mm				
		when struck		*	37	Æ	150
		when cast				Æ	35
	139.2	*The Church and The Seven Bishops.* Dutch medal, 58 mm			42	Æ	250
	139.3	*James II and Queen Mary.* Portraits, by G. Bower,	52 mm		45	Æ	450
	139.4	*Birth of Prince James* (later the Elder Pretender, 10 June). By G. Bower,	37 mm	*	46	Æ	600

Date	No.		Pic.	MI	Metal	Value
	139.5	*Birth of Prince James.* Likened to the infant Hercules, 30 mm	*	48	Æ	120
		● Other medals commemorating the birth were struck in Denmark and Holland.				
	139.6	*The Anti-Christian Confederacy.* Dutch medal, by J. Smeltzing, 38 mm		54	Æ	300
	139.7	*Invitation to William and Mary of Orange.* Dutch medal, 63 mm		58	Æ	250
	139.8	*Embarkation of William at Helvoetsluys.* Dutch medal, by O. Müller, 85 mm		59–60	Æ	—
	139.9	*The Landing of William at Torbay* (5 November). By G. Bower, 51 mm	*	64	Æ	150
		when cast			Æ	35
	139.10	*The Flight of Prince James (and Queen Mary).* By C. Wermuth, 32 mm		71	Æ	120
		● The infant Prince James is shown in the arms of a Jesuit, Father Petre, the King's confessor.				
	139.11	*The Abdication* (11 December). Medal struck 1788 during Jubilee of the Glorious Revolution, 38 mm		75	WM	25

HOUSE OF ORANGE AND STUART

William III and Mary II
(13 February 1689–28 December 1694)

William: Born 4 November 1650, Protestant nephew and son-in-law of James II, died 8 March 1702, after seven years as sole monarch. William was the elected Stadtholder of the United Provinces.

Mary: Born 30 April 1662, elder surviving daughter of James II (and Anne Hyde), and wife of William III, died 28 December 1694.

William III was a monarch of two countries and the Dutch influence on English medals now becomes more and more obvious. *Medallic Illustrations* lists many medals that relate to William III in name, but that have little connection with the events of English history. There were many medallists active in Holland and from the 'Landing at Torbay' and onwards into his English reign the output of medals was greater than any previous period of English history. The selection listed for the joint reign and for William III alone, has tried to concentrate on medals of English manufacture.

Date	No.			Pic.	MI	Metal	Value
1689	140.1	*Administration offered to William III.* Dutch medal, by J. Smeltzing,	48 mm	*	6	Æ	500
	140.2	*Louis XIV Receives James II.* French medal, by J. Mauger,	41 mm		8–9	Æ	25
	140.3	*The Church of England Restored.* By G. Bower,	52 mm *usually cast*		18	Æ	85
	140.4	*Rebellion in Ireland.* Dutch medal by J. Luder,	52 mm		24	Æ	—
	140.5	*Coronation.* The official medal, by J. Roettier,	32 mm (515 specimens struck) (1,200 specimens struck)	*	25	A/ Æ	1250 120
	140.6	*Coronation.* By G. Bower. ℞ Perseus and Andromeda,	37 mm		26	Æ	100
	140.7	*Coronation.* By G. Bower. ℞ William and Mary below canopy of state,	55 mm *Usually cast*	*	38	Æ	100
	140.8	*The Security of Britain.* German medal, by P. H. Müller,	55 mm	*	60	Æ	300
		● This medal was struck at Nuremburg by F. Kleinert, a medallist who specialised in lettered edges, many of which, this included, he signed.					
	140.9	*The Act of Toleration.* German medal, by P. H. Muller,	50 mm		64	Æ	300
	140.10	*Londonderry Relieved.* Dutch medal,	44 mm	*	97	Æ	300
1690	141.1	*Mary, Proclaimed Regent.* By J. Roettier,	48 mm		111– 112	Æ	45

Date	No.		Pic.	MI	Metal	Value
	141.2	*William Arrives in Ireland.* Dutch medal, by J. Smeltzing, 48 mm		117	Æ	500
	141.3	*Action off Beachy Head.* French medal, by J. Mauger, 41 mm		121, 125–126	Æ	25
	141.4	*Mary as Regent, Lord Torrington Committed to the Tower* (after the Action off Beachy Head). Dutch medal, by J. Smeltzing, 37 mm		128–129	Æ	400
	141.5	*The Battle of the Boyne* (at which William himself led the charge of the Cavalry). Dutch medal, by R. Arondeaux, 48 mm	*	136–138	Æ	500
	141.6	*Amnesty in Ireland.* German medal, by G. Hautsch, 39 mm	*	146	Æ	200
1691	142.1	*William Lands in Holland.* Dutch medal, by F. Winter, 38 mm		156	Æ	—
	142.2	*Congress of the Allies at the Hague.* Dutch medal, by R. Arondeaux, 48 mm		181	Æ	600
	142.3	*Battle of Aghrim.* Dutch medal, by J. Smeltzing, 37 mm	*	205	Æ	300
	142.4	*Athlone, Galway and Sligo Taken.* Dutch medal, by J. Smeltzing, 50 mm		212–213	Æ	400
	142.5	*Limerick Taken.* Dutch medal, by J. Smeltzing, 56 mm	*	215	Æ	800
	142.6	*The Pacification of Ireland.* German medal, by G. Hautsch, 41 mm		224	Æ	200
	142.7	*Peace Restored.* German medal, by C. J. Leherr, 36 mm		233–234	Æ	200
1692	143.1	*Ireland Reunited.* Dutch medal, by J. Luder, 46 mm		241–242	Æ	300
	143.2	*Battle of La Hogue.* German medal, by G. Hautsch. Obverse as 141.6, ℞ Naval action, 39 mm ● *M.I.* lists 28 medals relating to the Battle of La Hogue when the combined English and Dutch fleets inflicted a severe defeat on the French.	*	258–259	Æ	250
	143.3	*Namur Taken.* French medal, by J. Mauger, 41 mm		276	Æ	35
	143.4	*Battle of Steinkirk, William III Defeated.* French medal, by J. Mauger, 41 mm		284	Æ	35
	143.5	*Battle of Steinkirk, William III Defeated.* Dutch medal, by J. Smeltzing, 56 mm		285	Æ	800
	143.6	*Execution of Barthelemi de Lignieres, Chevalier de Grandval* (hanged, drawn and quartered for planning to assassinate William III). Dutch medal by J. Boskam, 60 mm		287–288	Æ	—
1693	144.1	*John George IV, Elector of Saxony, Elected a Knight of the Garter.* German medal, by M. H. Omeis, 43 mm		292	Æ	500
	144.2	*Battle of Landen.* Dutch medal, by J. Boskam, 60 mm	*	303	Æ	800
1694	145.1	*Dieppe Bombarded by English.* Dutch medal, by J. Boskam, 50 mm		319–	Æ	800
	145.2	*Le Havre Bombarded by English.* Dutch medal, by J. Boskam. Obverse as 144.2, ℞ Brazen bull, 60 mm	*	321	Æ	1000
	145.3	*John Tillotson, Archbishop of Canterbury, Death.* From Dassier's set of medals of Reformers, early 18th century, 28 mm		331	Æ	20
	145.4	*Death of Queen Mary.* By James and N. Roettier, 50 mm	*	343	Æ	45
	145.5	*Death of Queen Mary.* Dutch medal, by J. Luder, 60 mm		345–346	Æ	120
	145.6	*Death of Queen Mary.* By James Roettier, 39 mm		364	Æ	60

William III
(sole monarch, 28 December 1694–8 March 1702)

For details of the King and a summary of the medallic situation during the reign see the introduction to William III and Mary II, above item 141.

Date	No.		Pic.	MI	Metal	Value
1695	146.1	*Casale Taken by the Allies.* Dutch medal, by J. Boskam, 37 mm		371–373	Æ	400
	146.2	*Brussels Bombarded and Namur Re-Taken.* Dutch medal, by M. Smeltzing, 50 mm	*	379	Æ	500
	146.3	*Assassination Plot* (by Sir George Barclay to murder William III at Turnham Green, West London). Dutch medal, busts of James II and Louis XIV, 43 mm		414	Æ	600
		New Coinage Introduced. No medal.				
1697	148.1	*The Peace of Ryswick* (France recognises William III and Princess Anne as his heir). German medal, by P. H. Müller, 46 mm		433	Æ	300
	148.2	*The Peace of Ryswick.* Dutch medal, by R. Arondeaux, 67 mm		454	Æ	350
	148.3	*The Peace of Ryswick.* Dutch jetton, by J. Luder, 20 mm ● *M.I.* lists 68 medals relating to the Peace and the Peace celebrations.		464	Æ	25
	148.4	*The State of Britain* (after the Peace of Ryswick). Fine portrait medal, by J. Croker (his first work), 69 mm	*	499	Æ	700
	148.5	*Prince James* (Elder Pretender). Small medals, by N. Roettier, 25 mm	*	500–504	Æ Æ	60 20
1699	150.1	*James II and Prince James.* By N. Roettier, 36 mm	*	515	Æ	150
	150.2	*Succession of Prince James.* Complimentary medal, by N. Roettier, 26 mm		519–	Æ	100
1700	151.1	*Storming of Toubucan in the Isthmus of Darien* (by Sir Alexander Campbell, for the proposed establishment of a colony). Dutch medal by M. Smeltzing, 56 mm	*	529	Æ	1500
1701	152.1	*Princesses Matilda and Sophia* (German medal to commemorate the line of accession to George I), following the death of the Duke of Gloucester. By S. Lambelet, 65 mm		542	Æ	450
1702	153.1	*Death of William III.* Dutch medal, by R. Arondeaux, 50 mm	*	547	Æ	275
	153.2	*Death of William III.* Dutch medal, by M. Smeltzing, 48 mm		550	Æ	250

HOUSE OF STUART

Anne
(8 March 1702–1 August 1714)
Born 6 February 1665, younger sister of Mary II,
daughter of James II (and Anne Hyde). Her
longest surviving child, the Duke of Gloucester,
died in 1700, aged twelve years.

The English medals produced during the reign of Queen Anne are strongly influenced by the work of one medallist, John Croker; but the major events and battles were often commemorated by a great number of European medals. This was the age of Marlborough and much of his tomb at Blenheim Palace is decorated with large marble replicas of Croker's medals.

Date	No.		Pic.	MI	Metal	Value
1702	153.3	*Accession*, 'ENTIRELY ENGLISH'. By J. Croker, 34 mm		1	Æ	65
	153.4	*Accession*, 'QUIS SEPARABIT'. By J. Croker, 36 mm		3	Æ	80
					Æ	35
	153.5	*Coronation*. The official medal, by J. Croker, 36 mm	*			
		(858 specimens struck)		4	A/	850
		(1,200 specimens struck)			Æ	80
	153.6	*Anne, and Prince George of Denmark* (who was created Captain-General of all forces and Lord High Admiral). Double portrait medal, by J. Croker, 42 mm	*	14	Æ	150
					Æ	80
	153.7	*Nimeguen Relieved from the French*. Dutch medal, by J. Boskam, 43 mm		15	Æ	250
	153.8	*Expedition to Vigo Bay* (the Spanish plate fleet captured and destroyed). By J. Croker, 37 mm	*	18	Æ	150
		● Many coins struck in 1702 are worded VIGO to signify that they were struck from captured bullion.				
	153.9	*Expedition to Vigo Bay*. Dutch medal, by J. Boskam, 43 mm		20	Æ	200
	153.10	*Capitulation of Liege and other towns on the Meuse*. By J. Croker, 37 mm	*	26	Æ	120
1703	154.1	*Bonn Taken by Marlborough*. Dutch medal, by J. Boskam, 43 mm		33	Æ	300
	154.2	*Bonn, Huy and Limbourg Taken by Marlborough*. By J. Croker, 42 mm	*	35	Æ	150
1704	155.1	*Queen Anne's Bounty*. By J. Croker, 44 mm		43	Æ	100
	155.2	*The Battle of Blenheim*. By J. Croker, 34 mm		49	Æ	100
					Æ	40

Date	No.		Pic.	MI	Metal	Value
	155.3	*The Battle of Blenheim*. By G. Hautsch (portrait of Marlborough), 37 mm	*	50	Æ\R	120
	155.4	*The Capture of Gibraltar and Naval Engagement off Malaga*. By J. Croker, 39 mm		64	Æ\R	150
	155.5	*John Locke, Philosopher, Death*. By J. Dassier, 42 mm		72	Æ	20
1705	156.1	*The French Lines forced in Brabant and Flanders*. Dutch medal, by J. Boskam, 43 mm	*	79	Æ\R	400
	156.2	*Barcelona Taken*. German medal, by P. H. Müller, 43 mm		83	Æ\R	250
1706	157.1	*Barcelona Relieved*. By J. Croker, 34 mm		86	Æ\R Æ	200 40
	157.2	*The Battle of Ramillies*. By J. Croker, 34 mm		92	Æ\R Æ	200 40
	157.3	*Victories of Anne over Louis XIV*. Dutch satirical medals, 43 mm	*	97–98	Æ\R	200
1707	158.1	*The Union of England and Scotland* (as a single Kingdom). By J. Croker, 47 mm	*	107	Æ\R	165
	158.2	*The Union of England and Scotland*. By J. Croker and S. Bull, 34 mm			A\/ Æ\R Æ	650 60 30
	158.3	*The Union of England and Scotland*. Larger medal, by J. Croker, 70 mm	*	115	Æ\R Æ	250 120
1708	159.1	*James III (The Elder Pretender), Restoration of the Kingdom*. By N. Roettier, 38 mm		133	Æ\R Æ	120 40
	159.2	*James III (The Elder Pretender), Restoration of the Kingdom*. By N. Roettier, 51 mm	*	135–136	Æ\R Æ	200 80
		● The Old Pretender landed in Scotland, but for only four days.				
	159.3	*Attempted Invasion of Scotland*. By J. Croker and S. Bull, 39 mm		141	Æ\R	80
	159.4	*Attempted Invasion of Scotland*. German medal, by G. Hautsch, 41 mm		142	Æ\R	150
	159.5	*The Battle of Oudenarde*. By J. Croker, 44 mm		148	Æ\R	200
	159.6	*The Capture of Sardinia and Minorca*. By. J. Croker, 39 mm		157	Æ\R	120
	159.7	*Death of Prince George of Denmark*. Danish medal, by M. Roeg, 50 mm		163	Æ\R	450
	159.8	*Citadel of Lille Taken*. By J. Croker, 43 mm	*	169	Æ\R	200
1709	160.1	*City of Tournai Taken*. By J. Croker, 39 mm		190	Æ\R	180
	160.2	*The Battle of Malplaquet*. By J. Croker, 47 mm	*	197	Æ\R	180
	160.3	*Mons Taken*. By J. Croker and S. Bull, 39 mm		202	Æ\R	160
1710	161.1	*Dr. Henry Sacheverell, Impeached*. 36 mm		210–211	Æ\R	80
	161.2	*Douay Taken*. By J. Croker, 48 mm	*	213	Æ\R	200
	161.3	*The Battle of Almenara*. By J. Croker, 48 mm		218	Æ\R	200
	161.4	*The Battle of Saragossa*. By J. Croker, 48 mm	*	219	Æ\R	200

Date	No.		Pic.	MI	Metal	Value
	161.5	*Capture of Bethune, St. Venant, and Aire.* By J. Croker and S. Bull, 48 mm		220	Æ	200
	161.6	*Successes of Prince Eugene and Marlborough.* German medal, by G. Hautsch, 44 mm		223	Æ	300
	161.7	*The Elder Pretender Claims the Throne.* By N. Roettier, 30 mm		229	Æ	40
1711	162.1	*The French Lines Passed and Bouchain Taken.* By J. Croker, 44 mm	*	237	Æ	150
	162.2	*The Concord of Britain.* German medal, by P. H. Müller, 43 mm		238	Æ	200
		Marlborough dismissed as Commander-in-chief. No medal.				
1712	163.1	*James III (The Elder Pretender) and Princess Louisa.* By N. Roettier, 52 mm	*	241	Æ	250
					Æ	80
	163.2	*Peace Congress at Utrecht.* Dutch medal, 71 mm		246	Æ	—
1713	164.1	*The Peace of Utrecht.* By J. Croker, 58 mm		256	Æ	200
	164.2	*The Peace of Utrecht.* Smaller medal, distributed (at public expense) in gold to members of the Houses of Parliament. By J. Croker, 34 mm	*	257	A/	600
					Æ	60
	164.3	*The Peace of Utrecht.* Dutch medal, by D. Drappentier, 48 mm		262	Æ	400
1714		*Death of Queen Anne. No contemporary medal.*				

HOUSE OF HANOVER

George I
(1 August 1714–11 June 1727)
Born 28 May 1660, great-grandson of James I,
and succeeded to the throne as a result of
the Act of Settlement excluding Catholics.

John Croker's influence continued into the reign of George I, and the German Court did not seem to introduce anything new, after Vestner's medals for the Accession. The early 18th century was a period of fairly prolific medal output in Germany, and the lack of evidence of this in England seems remarkable.

Date	No.			Pic.	MI	Metal	Value
1714	165.2	*Accession.* German medals, by G. Vestner,	43 mm		4–5	Æ	200
	165.3	*Arrival in England.* By J. Croker,	67 mm		6	Æ	220
						Æ	80
	165.4	*Entry into London.* By J. Croker,	47 mm	*	7	Æ	175
						Æ	60
	165.5	*Coronation.* The official medal. By J. Croker,	34 mm	*	9		
		(330 specimens struck)				A/	850
		(1,200 specimens struck)				Æ	80

● There was no Queen's Coronation medal. George had married his cousin Sophia Dorothea of Zell in 1683, but had divorced in 1694 on account of her adultery with the 'handsome adventurer', Count Königsmark. He was assassinated, but she lived on in seclusion and died in 1726.

Date	No.			Pic.	MI	Metal	Value
1715	166.1	*The Battle of Sheriffmuir or Dunblain* (the Jacobites, under the Earl of Mar, defeated). By J. Croker, 46 mm		*	33	Æ	120
						Æ	40
	166.2	*Preston Taken.* By J. Croker,	46 mm	*	34	Æ	120
						Æ	40
1716	167.1	*The Attempts of James III to Recover the English Throne* (1708 and 1716).		*	35	Æ	300
1717	168.1	*The Act of Grace and Free Pardon* (to those engaged in the rebellions). By J. Croker, 45 mm		*	36–37	Æ	200
1718	169.1	*Treaty of Passarowitz* (Morea retained by Turkey from Venice, George I mediator). By J. Croker,		*		Æ	180
						Æ	60
	169.2	*Death of William Penn, Founder of the State of Pennsylvania.* By L. Pingo (struck 1775), 40 mm		*	40	Æ	200
						Æ	60
	169.3	*Naval Action off Cape Passaro.* By J. Croker, 44 mm			42	Æ	160
	169.4	*Alliance of George I and the Emperor Charles VI.* By J. Dassier, 32 mm			46	Æ	80
	169.5	*Caroline (Wilhelmina Charlotte), Princess of Wales.* By J. Croker, 36 mm			47	Æ	100

Date	No.		Pic.	MI	Metal	Value
1719	170.1	*The Escape of Princess Clementina from Innsbruck* (she was imprisoned at the request of George I in an attempt to prevent her marriage (see item 170.2)). Italian medal, by O. Hamerani, 48 mm	*	49	Æ Æ	200 60
	170.2	*Marriage of James III, Elder Pretender and Princess Clementina.* Italian medal, by O. Hamerani, 40 mm		51	Æ Æ	150 80
	170.3	*Marriage of James III, Elder Pretender and Princess Clementina.* Larger Italian medal, by O. Hamerani, 48 mm		52	Æ Æ	250 80
1720	171.1	*John Law, Financier* (failure of the Mississippi Company and French national bankruptcy). By C. Wermuth, 34 mm		57– 58	Æ	400
	171.2	*Birth of Prince Charles Edward, The Young Pretender.* Italian medal, by O. Hamerani, 40 mm		60	Æ Æ	150 40
	171.3	*Birth of Prince Charles Edward, The Young Pretender.* By N. Roettier, 44 mm	*	61	Æ	75
		The 'South Sea Bubble' Bursts. No medal.				
1721	172.1	*James III, Elder Pretender, Appeal Against the House of Hanover.* Italian medal, by O. Hamerani, 51 mm	*	63	Æ	200
1722	173.1	*Death of John Churchill, Duke of Marlborough.* By J. Dassier, 42 mm	*	68	Æ Æ	150 40
1723	174.1	*Jacobite Conspiracy Discovered.* Satirical medal, 39 mm	*	70	Æ WM	— 200
1725	176.1	*The Order of the Bath Revived.* By J. Croker. ℞ Prince William (later Duke of Cumberland) in robes of the Order, 46 mm	*	75	Æ Æ	220 50
	176.2	*William Wake, Archbishop of Canterbury.* By J. Dassier, 43 mm	*	73	Æ Æ	75 20
1727	178.1	*Gibraltar Besieged by the Spanish,* 41 mm		82	Æ	300
	178.2	*Death of Sir Isaac Newton.* By J. Croker, 52 mm		83	Æ	35
	178.3	*Death of Sir Isaac Newton.* Small medal, by J. Dassier, 33 mm		84	Æ	35
	178.4	*Death of Sir Isaac Newton.* Larger medal, by J. Dassier, 43 mm	*	85	Æ	35
	178.5	*Death of George I.* By J. Dassier, 32 mm	*	92	Æ	50

George II
(11 June 1727–25 October 1760)
Born 30 October 1683, only son of George I.

The German and continental influence is very much shown by the listing of the medals of the reign in *Medallic Illustrations*. George II is remembered as the last monarch to lead his troops into battle, at Dettingen in 1743, but most medals for this event are extremely rare. The victories late in his reign, in India and the Americas are, however, more represented on medals.

Date	No.		Pic.	MI	Metal	Value
1727	178.6	*Coronation.* The official medal. By J. Croker, 34 mm (238 specimens struck) (800 specimens struck)	*	4	AV Æ	1000 75

Date	No.		Pic.	MI	Metal	Value
	178.7	*Coronation, Queen Caroline.* The official medal. By J. Croker, 34 mm	*	8		
		(138 specimens struck)			AV	1200
		(400 specimens struck)			AR	75
		● The availability of this medal does not tally with the low mintage figure that has been published.				
1728	179.1	*John Friend*, F.R.S., and sometime M.P.. Italian medal, by F. St. Urbain, 58 mm		28	Æ	50
1729	180.1	*Frederick, Created Prince of Wales.* By J. Dassier, 41 mm		29	Æ	40
	180.2	*Death of Dr. Samuel Clarke*, mathematician and philosopher. By J. Dassier, 42 mm			Æ	20
	180.3	*Prince Charles, The Young Pretender, and his Brother Prince Henry.* Italian medal, by O. Hamerani, 42 mm		34	AR Æ	120 40
	180.4	*Prince Charles, The Young Pretender, and his Brother Prince Henry.* Larger Italian medal, by O. Hamerani, 46 mm		35	AR Æ	200 60
1731	182.1	*The Second Treaty of Vienna* (between England, Holland, Spain and the Holy Roman Empire). By J. Croker, 47 mm	*	39	AR Æ	180 60
	182.2	*George II, Dassier's Dedication Medal* (to his series of medals depicting the Kings and Queens of England from William I), 41 mm		43	Æ	25
	182.3	*Queen Caroline*, the companion medal, 41 mm		44	Æ	25
		● The set of 33 medals depicting the monarchs since William I was offered for sale (in copper) for 6 guineas. The individual medals have not been listed elsewhere in this catalogue but are common in copper and have a catalogue value of £10–£15.				
	182.4	*The State of Britain.* German medal, by G. Vestner, 43 mm		46	AR	200
1732	183.1	*The Royal Family*, portrait medal. By J. Croker. R busts of the seven royal children, by J. Tanner, 70 mm	*	47	AR Æ	350 70
1733	184.1	*Death of Matthew Tindall* (author, 1730, of 'Christianity as Old as the Creation'), 50 mm	*	50	AR Æ	150 50
1734	185.1	*Marriage of William, Prince of Orange and Princess Anne.* Dutch medal, by N. van Swinderen, 47 mm		57	AR	150
	185.2	*Marriage of William, Prince of Orange and Princess Anne.* Dutch medal, by M. Holtzhey, 44 mm; 29 mm	*	55, 58– 60	AR	60
1736	187.1	*Frederick, Prince of Wales, marriage to Princess Augusta of Saxony.* German medal, by G. Vestner, 44 mm	*	69– 70	AR	150
	187.2	*Henry Jernegan's Lottery Medal* (for a magnificent, large silver cistern – a medal being given to each person purchasing a ticket – and 30,000 were struck). By S. Tanner, 38 mm	*	72	AR	15
	187.3	*Death of John Conduit* (M.P. and Master of the Mint). By S. Tanner, 58 mm		73	AR Æ	150 40
1737	188.1	*Death of Queen Caroline.* German medallic Thaler, 41 mm	*	80	AR	150
	188.2	*John Milton* (on the erection of his monument in Westminster Abbey). By S. Tanner, 52 mm		83	AR Æ	100 35
1738	189.1	*Dean Jonathon Swift* (author of Gulliver's Travels). Irish medal, signed I.R., 41 mm	*	86	AR	250

Date	No.		Pic.	MI	Metal	Value
1739	190.1	*The Anstruther Beggar's Benison Club Founded* (an outlet 'for exuberant and outrageous fun . . . of the roughest description'). Members' badge, 36 × 29 mm	*	87–88	Æ gilt	100
	190.2	*Convention of Prado* (Spanish reimburse British merchants for war damages), 30 mm		90–91	Æ	40
	190.3	*Porto Bello Captured by Admiral Vernon* ('with six ships only'), *Average* 41 mm	*	92–138	Æ	20
		● Admiral Vernon had boasted that Porto Bello, a Spanish possession, could be captured 'with six ships only' and as he was successful the event became a popular cause for celebration with the production, for the first time in England, of large numbers of cheap medals. They were issued by a clock, watch and toy maker, one Edward Pinchbeck and struck in the gold-looking copper-zinc alloy that his father had invented and given his name to. When new they must have looked splendid, but are now hard to find in this condition; poor specimens are excessively common.				
1740	191.1	*Fort Chagre (Castle St. Lorenzo) Captured by Admiral Vernon.* Similar medals, *Average* 41 mm	*	139–154	Æ	20
	191.2	*Martin Folkes*, Antiquarian and Numismatist. By J. A. Dassier, 55 mm	*	185	Æ	40
		● The first of a set of 13 medals of famous men in England.				
	191.3	*Birth of Princess Elizabeth Caroline.* German medal, by J. Koch, 44 mm		186	Æ	85
	191.4	*Admiral Vernon and the Duke of Argyle,* 41 mm		188–189	Æ	20
		● Items 191.4–192.2 are similar in manufacture to items 190.30–192.1.				
1741	192.1	*Carthagena Taken by Admiral Vernon.* Similar to the Porto Bello medals, *Average* 41 mm		155–176	Æ	20
	192.2	*Admiral Vernon and Sir Robert Walpole,* 30 mm		192	Æ	25
	192.3	*Sir Robert Walpole.* By L. Natter, 48 mm	*	193	Æ	150
	192.4	*Alexander Pope*, Poet. By J. A. Dassier, 55 mm		198	Æ	40
1742	193.1	*Sir Robert Walpole, Earl of Orford* (he had been compelled to resign the office of Prime Minister). By L. Natter, 39 mm		201	Æ	85
	193.2	*Charles, Duke of Marlborough.* By J. A. Dassier, 55 mm		202	Æ	30
	193.3	*Monument to Princess Clementina* (in St. Peter's, Rome). Papal medal of Benedict XIV, 34 mm	*	204	Æ Æ	120 30
	193.4	*Martin Folkes* (in Rome). Italian medal, 37 mm		206	Æ	30
		● See also item 191.2.				
1743	194.1	*Birth of Princess Caroline.* Dutch medal, by N. van Swinderen, 47 mm		207	Æ	120
	194.2	*The Battle of Dettingen.* German medal, by M. Hannibal, 56 mm		213	Æ	800
		● This was the last battle where the English troops were commanded in action by the monarch. The King was accompanied by his son, the Duke of Cumberland.				
	194.3	*The Battle of Dettingen.* By T. Tibs (?) 'cheap' medal, 35 mm	*	215	Æ	40

Date	No.		Pic.	MI	Metal	Value
	194.4	*John Campbell, Duke of Argyle.* By J. A. Dassier, 55 mm		216	Æ	35
	194.5	*Marriage of Prince Frederick of Denmark to Princess Louisa* (youngest daughter of George II). Danish medal, by G. Wahl (given to all present at the celebration banquet), 65 mm		219	Æʀ	300
	194.6	*Philip Stanhope, Earl of Chesterfield.* By J. A. Dassier, 55 mm		222		35
1744	195.1	*Naval Action off Toulon.* 'Cheap' medal, 41 mm		224	Æ	15
	195.2	*Sir Robert Walpole, Earl of Orford.* By J. A. Dassier, 55 mm		226	Æ	40
	195.3	*John, Lord Carteret*, politician. By J. A. Dassier, 55 mm		228	Æ	35
	195.4	*William Polteney, Earl of Bath*, politician. By J. A. Dassier, 55 mm		229	Æ	35
	195.5	*Sir John Barnard.* By J. A. Dassier, 55 mm		230	Æ	35
	195.6	*Robert Barker*, Physician. By J. A. Dassier, 55 mm		232	Æ	50
	195.7	*Sir Hans Sloane*, Physician and Collector. By J. A. Dassier, 55 mm		234	Æ	50
	195.8	*Edmund Halley*, Mathematician and Astronomer. By J. A. Dassier (Halley had died in 1742), 55 mm	*	235	Æ	60
	195.9	*Sir Andrew Fountaine*, Warden of the Mint. By J. A. Dassier, 55 mm		236	Æ	40
	195.10	*Charles, Prince of Lorraine Recaptures Prague* (from Frederick the Great, helped by British subsidies to Hungary). By J. Kirk, 43 mm	*	237–238	Æ	50
	195.11	*Charles, Prince of Lorraine Recaptures Prague.* Unsigned variety, Charles on horseback, 42 mm		239	Æ	10
1745	196.1	*Arrival of the Young Pretender Expected* (AMOR ET SPES), 42 mm	*	251	Æʀ	65
					Æ	25
	196.2	*Prince Charles Edward, The Young Pretender*, 36 mm		256	Æ	40
	196.3	*Carlisle Taken* (by William, Duke of Cumberland). German medal, by J. Wolff, 37 mm		258–259	Æʀ	60
					Æ	25
	196.4	*Carlisle Taken.* 'Cheap' medal issued by Pinchbeck, 34 mm		262	Æ	15
	196.5	*The Rebels Repulsed.* By A. Kirk, 34 mm		264	Æʀ	35
					Æ	20
	196.6	*The Rebels Repulsed.* ℞ Lion and Wolf. By T. Pingo, 33 mm		265	Æʀ	30
	196.7	*The Rebels Repulsed.* George II receives Cumberland. By J. and A. Kirk, 41 mm	*	267–268	Æʀ	120
					Æ	40
	196.8	*The Rebels Repulsed.* By J. Kirk (2 ℞ designs), 29 mm		269–270	Æ	30
1746	197.1	*The Battle of Culloden.* German medal, by J. Wolff, 41 mm	*	271	Æʀ	50
	197.2	*The Battle of Culloden.* By J. Kirk, 43 mm		172–273	Æʀ	70
					Æ	30
	197.3	*The Battle of Culloden.* Cumberland 'British Hero', 36 mm		274	Æ	15
		● *M.I.* lists three other varieties of similar 'Pinchbeck' medals, all of which are common in poor condition and of the same value.				
	197.4	*The Battle of Culloden.* Portrait medal of Cumberland. By R. Yeo, 51 mm	*	278	AV	1500
					Æʀ	200
					Æ	50
	197.5	*Rebellion Defeated.* ℞ Supliant Scot, 32 mm		285–286	Æ	15

Date	No.		Pic.	MI	Metal	Value
	197.6	*Execution of Rebels.* ℞ A rebel hanged, 33 mm		289	Æ	45
	197.7	*Failure of Prince Charles.* ℞ 'Come Back Again', 33 mm		290	Æ	25
1747	198.1	*William of Orange Created Stadtholder* (of the United Provinces). Dutch medal, by M. Holtzhey, 43 mm		314	AR	200
	198.2	*William of Orange Created Stadtholder* (of the United Provinces). 'Cheap' medal, 41 mm		323	Æ	10
	198.3	*Admiral George, Lord Anson.* French fleet defeated off Cape Finisterre and his voyage around the world, 1740–1744. By T. Pingo, 43 mm	*	325	AV AR Æ	1500 120 60
	198.4	*Defeat of the French Fleet off Cape Finisterre.* Pinchbeck type medal, *M.I.* pl. CLXXI/7 41 mm		—	Æ	30
1748	199.1	*Peace of Aix-la-Chapelle Concluded.* Dutch medal, by M. Holtzhey, 34 mm		342	AR	80
	199.2	*Peace of Aix-la-Chapelle Concluded.* By J. Kirk (portrait of George II), 34 mm	*	354	AR Æ	80 30
1749	200.1	*Dissentions of Dr. Charles Lucas and the Corporation of Dublin.* By T. Pingo, 39 mm		357	Æ	100
	200.2	*Prince Charles, 'Highlander medal'.* ℞ rose, 32 mm	*	358	Æ	75
1750	201.1	*Prince Charles, 'Oak Medal'* of a Jacobite Society. By T. Pingo, 34 mm	*	359	AR Æ	100 40
	201.2	*Prince Charles.* Larger portrait medal. By T. Pingo (but found only as early 19th-century restrikes), 51 mm	*	360	Æ	100
	201.3	*The State of England.* By J. A. Dassier, 55 mm		363	Æ	60
	201.4	*Free British Fishery Society* (Prince Frederick). German medal, by L. Koch, 41 mm		365	AR Æ	80 30
	201.5	*Frederick, Prince of Wales*, portrait. By J. A. Dassier, 55 mm		366	Æ	60
1751	202.1	*Death of Frederick, Prince of Wales.* By J. Kirk, 36 mm		367	AR Æ	120 40
	202.2	*Free British Fishery Society* (George, Prince of Wales). By J. Kirk, 36 mm		368	Æ	45
	202.3	*John, Duke of Montagu.* By J. A. Dassier, 55 mm	*	369	Æ	45
	202.4	*George II, Cambridge University Chancellor's Medal.* By R. Yeo, 51 mm		377	Æ	65
1752	203.1	*Visit of Prince Charles to London.* By T. Pingo, 43 mm	*	380	AR	85
		● When told of the visit, in September 1752, the King stated that 'when he is tired of England he will go abroad again' – and he did. *Gregorian Calendar adopted by Great Britain. No medal.*				
1753	204.1	*Edinburgh Revolution Club,* 36 mm (often gilt)		384	AR	85
	204.2	*Irish Surplus Revenue Dispute.* Medal for wearing, 44 mm	*	385	Æ	100
		● The Irish Parliament rejected a bill enabling them to appropriate surplus revenue, as the King of England's consent had been added to it.				
	204.3	*Irish Surplus Revenue Dispute.* Henry Boyle, Speaker, 36 mm		386	Æ	60
1755	206.1	*Earl of Kildare and Irish Surplus Revenue Dispute,* 36 mm		391	Æ	60
	206.2	*The Louth (Ireland) Election,* 44 mm	*	392	AR	175
1756	207.1	*The Loss of Minorca,* 'cheap' medal, of General Blakeney and Admiral Byng, 36 mm	*	394– 395	Æ	25

Date	No.		Pic.	MI	Metal	Value
1757	208.1	*The Abundant Harvest*, 'cheap' medal, 27 mm		397	Æ	20
	208.2	*Eddystone Lighthouse rebuilt* (badge for workmen to prevent them being press-ganged into the Navy), 43 mm	*	399	AR	500
	208.3	*General Clive, Victory at Plassey.* S.P.A.C. medal, by J. Pingo 39 mm		400	AR / Æ	100 / 35
		● The Royal Society for Promoting Arts and Commerce sponsored the striking of a number of medals during the war with France. These are referred to in the text by the initials S.P.A.C. Some of these medals may be found with the lettered edge, 'WILLIAM PITT ADMINISTRING', and these are now considered quite rare.				
	208.4	*The Battles of Rosbach and Lissa.* Frederick the Great, of Prussia, 'cheap' medals, 25–48 mm		402–403	Æ	15
		● There are many more medals for these battles, but with German legends. They again were cheaply produced and are still plentiful.				
1758	209.1	*Louisburg (Canada) Taken.* Award medal, by T. Pingo, 43 mm	*	404	AV / AR / Æ	— / 350 / 75
	209.2	*Louisburg Taken.* S.P.A.C. medal. By J. Pingo, 40 mm		405–407	AR / Æ	320 / 125
	209.3	*Louisburg Taken.* Admiral Boscawen, 'cheap' medals, 37 mm (and smaller)		408–	Æ	25
	209.4	*Goree Taken.* S.P.A.C. medal. By J. Pingo, 40 mm	*	415	AR / Æ	120 / 45
	209.5	*George II, Military and Naval Successes of 1758,* 44 mm		416	Æ	20
1759	210.1	*Death of George Frederick Handel,* composer. *No contemporary medal.*				
	210.2	*Guadaloupe Taken.* S.P.A.C. medal, by L. Pingo, 40 mm		427	AR / Æ	150 / 65
	210.3	*Majority of George, Prince of Wales.* Portrait medal, by T. Pingo, 55 mm	*	428	AR / Æ	200 / 50
	210.4	*The Battle of Minden.* S.P.A.C. medal, by J. Pingo, 40 mm		431	AR / Æ	120 / 45
	210.5	*The Battle of Minden, Prince Ferdinand of Brunswick-Wolfenbuttel.* By J. Kirk, 36 mm		433	AR / Æ	120 / 40
	210.6	*The Marquess of Granby* (Gallant conduct at Minden). 'Cheap' medal, 27 mm		436	Æ	20
	210.7	*Quebec Taken.* S.P.A.C. medal, by J. Pingo, 40 mm		439	AR / Æ	225 / 100
	210.8	*Death of General James Wolfe,* at Quebec. By J. Kirk, 37 mm		440	Æ	150
	210.9	*George II, Military and Naval Successes of 1759,* 34 mm		442–444	AR / Æ	85 / 25
	210.10	*George II, Successes of 1758–59.* Non-portrait, 34 mm	*	445	AR / Æ	75 / 20
1760	211.1	*Montreal Taken and the Conquest of Canada.* S.P.A.C. medal, by J. Kirk, 41 mm	*	447	AR / Æ	150 / 75
	211.2	*Canada Subdued.* S.P.A.C. medal, by L. Pingo, 38 mm		448	AR / Æ	150 / 75
	211.3	*Death of George II.* By J. Dassier, 42 mm	*	454	Æ	75

George III
(25 October 1760–29 January 1820)
Born 4 June 1738, eldest son of Frederick, Prince of Wales (eldest son of George II, died 1751)

The reign of George III saw the introduction of the steam press by Matthew Boulton and the industry of this one man was to establish the possibility of mass-producing medals for a much wider market. At the turn of the 19th Century one family, the Wyon's, began an influence on English medals that was to last a century. Historically the reign began with war against France and the later wars at sea and in the Spanish Peninsular gave cause to many medals.

Date	No.			Pic	B.H.M.	Metal	Value
1760	211.4	*Accession.* By T. Pingo,	55mm	·	1	Æℝ	250
	211.5	*Accession.* By T. Pingo. ℞ Britannia.	40mm		3	Æℝ	100
						Æ	40
	211.6	*The Arts Protected.* By T. Pingo,	39 mm	*	6	Æℝ	175
						Æ	60
1761	212.1	*Marriage to Charlotte* (Princess of Mecklenburg-Strelitz). By J. Kirk,	35 mm	*	10	Æℝ	60
	212.2	*Marriage to Charlotte.* Small counter, FELICITAS BRITANNIAE	26 mm		17	Æℝ	15
	212.3	*Coronation.* Official medal, by L. Natter,	34 mm	*	21–		
		(858 specimens struck)			24	AV	850
		(800 specimens struck)				Æℝ	125
	212.4	*Coronation, Queen Caroline.* Official medal, by L. Natter,	34 mm				
		(150 specimens struck)			66	AV	2000
		(400 specimens struck)				Æℝ	150
	212.5	*Coronation.* By T. Pingo,	40 mm		30	Æℝ	100
	212.6	*Coronation.* 'Cheap' medals.	25–34 mm			Æ	10
	212.7	*Belle Isle (Canada) Captured.* S.P.A.C. medal, by J. Kirk,	40 mm		70	Æℝ	85
						Æ	35
	212.8	*Pondicherry (India) Taken.* S.P.A.C. medal, by T. Pingo,	40 mm		72	Æℝ	120
						Æ	50
	212.9	*Marquis of Granby.* 'Cheap' medal.	34 mm		69	Æ	15
1762	213.1	*Queen Charlotte's Birthday.* Unsigned.	28 mm		74	Æℝ	100
	213.2	*Birth of George, Prince of Wales.* By T. Pingo,	40 mm	*	77	Æℝ	150
						Æ	40
	213.3	*Birth of George, Prince of Wales.* Unsigned. obv. as 213.1 ℞ Cherub.	28 mm		78	Æℝ	100
	213.4	*Events of the Year.* By J. Kirk,	40 mm		82	Æℝ	100
						Æ	40
1763	214.1	*The Princes George and Frederick.*	28 mm	*	84	Æℝ	45
						Æ	15
	214.2	*Birth of the Duke of Gloucester.*	25 mm		87	Æ	15
		Peace of Paris. No English medals.					
1764	215.1	*Prince Frederick, Bishop of Osnabruck.* By T. Pingo (issued 1765 on his 2nd birthday).	43 mm	*	90	Æℝ	70
						Æ	40
			40 mm			Æℝ	55
						Æ	25
			30 mm			Æℝ	30
						Æ	10

Date	No.		Pic	B.H.M.	Metal	Value
1765	216.1	*Death of Duke of Cumberland.* By J. van Noost, 38 mm	*	91	Æ	60
	216.2	*Marquis of Granby's Prize.* By T. Pingo (bust of George III). 37 mm		93	Æ	85
					Æ	40
		The Stamp Act Passed (for Taxing American Colonies). *No medal.*				
1766	217.1	*Robert (Lord) Clive.* By J. van Noost and I. Gosset, 41 mm	*	95	Æ	150
					Æ	60
	217.2	*Charles Pratt, Earl Camden, Lord Chancellor.* By T. Pingo, 40 mm		96	Æ	80
					Æ	35
	217.3	*Henry, Cardinal of York* (brother of Young Pretender). Italian medal, by F. Cropanese, 53 mm		99	Æ	150
					Æ	75
	217.4	*William Pitt, Repeal of Stamp Act.* By T. Pingo, 40 mm	*	100	Æ	150
					Æ	40
		● Sometimes unsigned, whilst another variety is signed I.W.				
	217.5	*Duke of Northumberland, Alnwick Castle.* By J. Kirk, 45 mm		106	Æ	65
1767	218.1	*The Royal College of Surgeons.* By T. Pingo, 45 mm	*	110	Æ	60
1768	219.1	*Duke of Grafton's Prize.* By J. Kirk (bust of George III). 54 mm		112	Æ	120
	219.2	*John Wilkes* (Middlesex Election). By J. Westwood (?), 40 mm		113	Æ	40
	219.3	*John Wilkes.* By J. Kirk, 35 mm	*	115	Æ	50
	219.4	*John Wilkes.* Unsigned. 45 mm		117	Æ	90
	219.5	*John Wilkes.* Medallets. @ 27 mm		118–125	Æ	15
	219.6	*Visit of Christian VII of Denmark.* By J. Kirk, 35 mm		127–128	Æ	40
	219.7	*Royal Academy Founded* (prize medal). By T. Pingo, 55 mm			Æ	250
1769	220.1	*Shakespeare Jubilee.* By J. Westwood, 36 mm	*		Æ	45
					Æ	25
		● David Garrick was a steward, and his initials DG are on the reverse of the medal.				
1770	221.1	*George III*, Laudatory Medal. By J. Kirk, 36 mm		137–138	Æ	150
					Æ	50
	221.2	*Death of William Beckford.* Unsigned. 42 mm		142	Æ	85
					Æ	40
	221.3	*Death of Marquis of Granby.* By L. Pingo, 40 mm	*	145	Æ	120
					Æ	40
	221.4	*Death of George Whitfield* (Methodist preacher). By T. Pingo, 36 mm		147	Æ	60
		● B.H.M. records 4 further medals. He died in America, at Newburyport, Mass.,				
		The Boston Massacre. No English medal.				
1771	222.1	*Armagh Library Opening*, J. Harrison. By J. Kirk, 37 mm		156	Æ	20
	222.2	*Armagh Library Opening*, Baron Rokeby. By J. Kirk, 37 mm	*	157	Æ	20
1772	223.1	*Death of Princess Augusta.* By T. Lyng, 33 mm		159	Æ	25
	223.2	*David Garrick.* By L. Pingo, 41 mm		160	Æ	40
	223.3	*David Garrick.* By J. Kirk, 41 mm		161	Æ	75

Date	No.		Pic	B.H.M.	Metal	Value
	223.4	*Prince Charles Edward* (Young Pretender), marriage to Princess Louisa. Unsigned. 32 mm	*	163	Æ Æ	120 25
	223.5	*Resolution and Adventure, Cook's Voyage.* Signed B.F. (struck by Matthew Boulton), 43 mm	*	165	Æ Æ	1500 750
1773	224.1	*George III*, portrait. Sentimental magazine issue. By J. Kirk, 26 mm		167	Æ	10
	224.2	*Queen Charlotte*, portrait. Sentimental magazine issue. By J. Kirk, 26 mm		168	Æ	10
	224.3	*Duke of Gloucester*, portrait. Sentimental magazine issue. By J. Kirk, 26 mm		169	Æ	10
	224.4– 224.9	*W. Beckford: D. Garrick: Duchess of Cumberland: Lord Chatham: Lord Camden: John Wilkes*; from the same series. By J. Kirk, each 26 mm		170– 182	Æ	10
	224.10	*Sir Joshua Reynolds.* By J. Kirk, 31 mm		177	Æ	45
	224.11	*St. Vincent's Rebellion.* By G. Moser, 56 mm	*	183	Æ	750
		Boston Tea Party. No medal.				
1774	225.1– 225.2	*Marquis of Granby: Duchess of Gloucester.* Sentimental magazine series. By J. Kirk, 26 mm		190, 194	Æ	10
	225.3	*William Hunter.* By E. Burch, 80 mm Variety issued by St. George's Hospital as a prize medal.		188	Æ Æ	150 150
	225.4	*Death of Duke of Atholl.* By J. Kirk,	*	192	Æ	70
		● In 1765 Atholl sold the sovereignty of the Isle of Man to the Treasury				
	225.5	*George III, Religious Stability.* By J. Kirk, 41 mm		197	Æ	45
1775	226.1	*George III, The Gold Re-Coinage.* By J. Kirk, 42 mm	*	202	Æ Æ	80 40
	226.2	*Lord North*, Chancellor at Oxford. By J. Kirk, 37 mm		200	Æ	40
1776	227.1	*David Garrick, Retirement.* By J. Kirk, 38 mm	*	204	Æ	50
	227.2	*George Washington, Siege of Boston.* French medal, by Du Vivier, *Usually re-strikes* 65 mm Original Restrike	*		Æ Æ	500 40
	227.3	*Benjamin Franklin.* By J. Kirk (unsigned and undated), 37 mm			Æ	75
		American Colonies Declaration of Independence. No medal.				
1777	228.1	*Battle of Germantown.* By J. Milton, (possibly a Military Reward for the 40th Regiment), 45 mm			Æ	400
	228.2	*Horatio Gates, Saratoga Springs.* French medal, by N. Gatteaux, *Usually re-strikes* 56 mm Original Restrike			Æ Æ	250 40
	228.3	*'Le Chevalier' d'Eon*, Statesman and famous transvestite, portrait. By J. Kirk, ℞ legend. 41 mm	*		Æ	85
		● 'Le Chevalier' d'Eon was an amazing personality who lived a long time in London, dying there in 1810.				
1778	229.1	*Death of William Pitt, Earl of Chatham.* By J. Kirk, 38 mm	*	213	Æ	45
	229.2	*Admiral Keppel, Battle of Ushant.* Signed I.H. 41 mm		214	Æ	40

Date	No.			Pic	B.H.M.	Metal	Value
1779	230.1	*Death of Captain Cook*. Unsigned.	39 mm	*	218–219	WM	75
	230.2	*Admiral Keppel, Acquitted*. By T. Lyng,	33 mm		220–221	Æ	45
	230.3	*John Paul Jones, Capture of the Serapis*. French medal, by A. Dupré, *Usually re-strikes* 57 mm			222	Æ	25
1780	231.1	*Admiral Rodney, Battle of Cape St. Vincent*. Signed A. 38 mm		*	225	Æ	45
	231.2	*The 'Gordon' Riots*. By T. Spence,	30 mm		227	Æ	30
1781	232.1	*Admiral Rodney, Capture of St. Eustatius*. Unsigned. 34 mm			230–236	Æ	40
	232.2	*Admiral Rodney, Capture of St. Eustatius*. Unsigned. 24 mm			237–238	Æ	30
	232.3	*Battle of Cowpens*. French medal, by Du Vivier, *Usually re-strikes* 47 mm				Æ	25
	232.4	*George III, War with America*. Unsigned,	53 mm		239	AR	—
	232.5	*Trial of Lord George Gordon*. Unsigned.	44 mm	*	240	Æ	40
1782	233.1	*Thomas Ryder*, Actor. By W. Mossop,	44 mm	*	242	Æ	30
	233.2	*Admiral Rodney, Battle of 12th April*.	24 mm		244	Æ	40
	233.3	*General Eliott, Siege of Gibraltar*. By Terry,	42 mm		246	AR	80
	233.4	*Siege of Gibraltar*. Eliott's medal. By L. Pingo,	49 mm		248	AR	200
1783	234.1	*Majority of George, Prince of Wales*. Unsigned.	32 mm		250	Æ	60
	234.2	*Relief of Gibraltar*. Picton's medal. By L. Pingo,	59 mm	*	253	AR	350
1783	234.3	*American Independence*. Unsigned.	40 mm		256	WM	—
	234.4	*Joseph Priestley*, Chemist. By J. Hancock,	36 mm	*	251	Æ	35
1784	235.1	*George, Prince of Wales*, Birthday. Unsigned.	38 mm		257	WM	50
	235.2	*Captain Cook*, Royal Society medal. By L. Pingo, 44 mm		*	258	AR / Æ	500 / 200
	235.3	*George Frederick Handel*, Centenary concerts. Unsigned. 32 mm			259	AR	40
	235.4	*Vincent Lunardi*, first balloon flight in England. Unsigned. 35 mm		*	260	Æ / WM	80 / 50

235.4 ● Probably issued when the balloon was exhibited at the Pantheon Theatre, Oxford Street.

Death of Samuel Johnson. No medal.

Date	No.			Pic	B.H.M.	Metal	Value
1785	236.1	*American Independence*, John Adams ambassador in London. By J. Pingo, 40 mm		*	265	Æ	75
	236.2	*George III, Gottingen University*. By E. Burch,	51 mm		266	AR	80
1786	237.1	*The Earl of Charlemont*, Royal Irish Academy medal. By W. Mossop, 53 mm		*	267	AR / Æ	250 / 75
1787	238.1	*Adam Smith*, Economist and author. By J. Milton (?) 40 mm			268	AR / Æ	150 / 50
1788	239.1	*George III, Visit to Cheltenham*. Signed R.W.	28 mm		271–272	Æ	10
	239.2	*George III, Visit to Worcester*. Several makers.	25 mm		273–277	Æ	10
	239.3	*Queen Charlotte*, laudatory medal. By Wilmore, Alston & Co., 25 mm			278–279	Æ	15

Date	No.		Pic	B.H.M.	Metal	Value
	239.4	*Henry IX, Cardinal York* (adoption of the title on the death of Charles Edward Stuart). Italian medal, by G. Hamerani, 53 mm	*	282	Æ Æ	150 70
	239.5	*George III, Gottingen University.* By E. Burch, 55 mm		291	Æ Æ	120 50
		Trial of Warren Hastings. No medal.				
1789	240.1	*George III, Recovery from Illness.* By J. Davies and others. 21–33 mm		294– 300, 302– 310	Æ WM	15 10
	240.2	*George III, Recovery from Illness.* By Droz (and Boulton). 35 mm	*	311	Æ Æ	50 15
	240.3	*George III, Recovery from Illness,* St. Paul's Thanksgiving. By L. Pingo, 54 mm		312– 313	Æ	75
	240.4	*George III, Recovery from Illness,* Cheltenham Celebrations. By J. Hancock, 44 mm		301	Æ	60
	240.5	*George III, Royal Visits.* Lyndhurst: Southampton: Weymouth: Bath. By J. Davies and others. Mostly Æ,22–33 mm		314– 320	Æ	15
	240.6	*George, Prince of Wales, Regent.* By R. Dixon, 27–30 mm		321– 322	Æ	15
	240.7	*Charles James Fox,* politician. Medallets. 35 mm		323– 325	Æ	15
	240.8	*William Pitt,* statesman. Medallets. 34 mm		326– 329	Æ	15
	240.9	*Doctor (Rev. Francis) Willis.* By C. James and T. Wyon, 33 mm	*	333	WM	20
		● Willis ran a private asylum in Lincolnshire. In December 1788 he had been called on to attend the King in his madness.				
	240.10	*John Wesley, 50th Year of Methodism.* By W. Mainwaring, 36 mm		334– 337	WM	30
	240.11	*Richard Brinsley Sheridan,* Dramatist and politician. Unsigned. 35 mm		346	WM	30
1790	241.1	*George III and Queen Charlotte.* By T. Wyon, 22 mm	*	338, 340	Æ	15
	241.2	*Manchester Church and King Club.* By L. Pingo, 45 mm *Often found glazed.*	*	344	Æ	60
1791	242.1	*Marriage of Frederick, Duke of York.* By F. Loos, 46 mm		348	Æ	50
	242.2	*Marriage of Frederick, Duke of York.* By W. Mainwaring, 38 mm		349	Æ	30
	242.3	*Death of Lord Effingham.* By J. Milton, 35 mm		353	Æ Æ	55 25
	242.4	*Death of John Wesley.* By J. Hancock, 39 mm		357	Æ	30
	242.5	*Death of John Wesley.* By W. Mainwaring, 36 mm	*	358– 359	WM	15
1792	243.1	*George, Prince of Wales,* tribute. 48 mm		361	Æ	150
	243.2	*Cornwallis, Defeat of Sultan Tipoo.* By C. H. Küchler. 48 mm	*	363	Æ Æ	120 40
		● Examples of this medal are found dated 1793, in error, but are of the same value.				
1793	244.1	*Thomas Paine,* revolutionary. Unsigned. 33 mm	*	365	WM	25

Date	No.		Pic	B.H.M.	Metal	Value
	244.2	*The Duke of York, Valenciennes Surrenders.* By W. Mainwaring, 39 mm		368	WM	15
	244.3	*George III, King and Constitution.* By C. Twigg, 37 mm		370	WM	15
1794	245.1	*Thomas Erskine and Vicary Gibbs.* By J. Milton, 44 mm		376	Æ̷ Æ	125 50
	245.2	*Tooke, Thelwall and Hardy,* acquitted of Treason. Unsigned. 37 mm		377	WM	25
1794	245.3	*Earl Howe, 'Glorious First of June'.* By C. H. Küchler, 47 mm	*	383	Æ̷ Æ	150 35
	245.4	*Earl Howe, 'Glorious First of June'.* By W. Wyon. 41 mm ● This is the first of the series of National Medals issued by J. Mudie in 1820, but they each are listed in sequence for the date of the event they commemorate.	*	387	Æ	15
1795	246.1	*Queen Charlotte's Birthday,* (Frogmore) By C. H. Küchler, 34 mm ● The reverse is also used with an obverse of George III, by Droz.	*	389	Æ̷	40
	246.2	*Marriage of George, Prince of Wales,* to Princess Caroline of Brunswick. By C. H. Küchler, 48 mm ● Dated, in error, 1797.	*	392	Æ	40
	246.3	*Marriage of George, Prince of Wales,* to Princess Caroline of Brunswick. Medallets. 26–36 mm		394– 400	Æ	15
	246.4	*Lord Stanhope,* 'Friend of Juries'. By W. Whitley, 42 mm	*	405	WM	25
	246.5	*Admiral Hood, Action off Isle de Groix.* By J. Hancock, 49 mm		406	Æ̷	90
		Warren Hastings acquitted. No medal.				
1796	247.1	*Birth of Princess Charlotte.* 22 mm		409	Æ̷ Æ	20 10
	247.2	*Sir Henry Trollope, Action off Helvoetsluys,* By J. Hancock, 48 mm	*	414	Æ	40
	247.3	*York Minster, (Cliffords Tower).* By T. Wyon, 45 mm		418	Æ̷ Æ	50 20
	247.4	*Missionary Ship Duff,* "To The South Seas". 37 mm	*		WM	50
1797	248.1	*Maj. General Claude Martin.* By McKenzie, 34–38 mm	*	424	Æ̷ Æ	75 30
	248.2	*French fleet in Bantry Bay.* By W. Mossop, 39 mm		425	Æ̷ Æ	150 50
	248.3	*Admiral Adam Duncan, Battle of Camperdown.* By J. Hancock, 47 mm		426	Æ	40
	248.4	*Admiral Adam Duncan, Battle of Camperdown.* By T. Wyon, 39 mm	*	428	Æ WM	40 20
	248.5	*Admiral Adam Duncan, Battle of Camberdown.* By T. Webb and W. Wyon (Mudie's medal), 41 mm		432	Æ	15
	248.6	*Admiral Sir Richard Onslow.* By J. Hancock, 47 mm	*	427	Æ	60
	248.7	*Admiral Jervis, (Earl St. Vincent) Battle of Cape St. Vincent.* By T. Wyon, 38 mm		433	Æ WM	30 15
	248.8	*Admiral Jervis, (Earl St. Vincent) Battle of Cape St. Vincent.* By G. Mills & N. Brenet (Mudie's medal), 41 mm	*	438	Æ	15
	248.9	*Howe, St. Vincent, Duncan, Thanksgiving at St. Pauls.* 32 mm			Æ	15
1798	249.1	*John Philip Kemble,* actor. By J. Hancock, 36 mm		446	Æ	30

Date	No.			Pic	B.H.M.	Metal	Value
	249.2	*John Philip Kemble*, actor. Larger variety.	56 mm			Æ	65
	249.3	*Battle of the Nile* (Davison's medal). By C. H. Küchler,	46 mm		447	Æ̷	150
						Æ	60
	249.4	*Battle of the Nile.* By J. Hancock and P. Kempson.	47 mm		448	Æ	60
	249.5	*Battle of the Nile.* Unsigned.	38 mm		452	Æ	35
						WM	15
	249.6	*Admiral Sir John Borlase Warren, Action off Tory Island.* By J. Hancock,	49 mm		455	Æ	60
	249.7	*George III, Victories of the Year.* By C. H. Küchler,	48 mm	*	458	Æ	40
	249.8	*Birmingham Loyal Association.* By J. S. Jorden,	41 mm		459	Æ	30
	249.9	*Matthew Boulton's Coinage machinery.* By R. Dumarest,	43 mm		462	Æ	60
		Death of George Vancouver, explorer and navigator. No medal.						
1799	250.1	*Death of Earl Howe.* By T. Wyon,	38 mm		468	Æ	25
						WM	10
	250.2	*William Pitt.* By J. Hancock,	54 mm		470	Æ	30
	250.3	*Earl Spencer.* By T. Wyon,	38 mm		471	Æ	25
						WM	10
	250.4	*Sir William Sidney Smith*, Defence of Acre. By J. Hancock,	48 mm	*	473	Æ	50
	250.5	*Sir William Sidney Smith*, Defence of Acre. By G. Mills and N. Brenet (Mudie's medal),	41 mm		476	Æ	15
	250.6	*Sir Ralph Abercromby, Capture of Helder Point.* Unsigned.	39 mm		477	Æ	25
	250.7	*Marquis Wellesley, Capture of Seringapatam.* By G. Mills and N. Brenet (for Mudie, but not used in series).	41 mm		479	Æ	25
		● The E.I.Co. medal (by Küchler) for this event was a military reward.						
	250.8	*Ferdinand IV, Re-established as King of the Two Sicilies* (by Nelson). By C. H. Küchler,	46 mm		479	Æ̷	150
						Æ	50
1800	251.1	*George III, Assasination attempt.* By C. H. Küchler,	48 mm		482–485	Æ	50
	251.2	*George III, Assasination attempt.* By P. Kempson,	38 mm	*	486	Æ̷	35
						Æ	15
						WM	10
	251.3	*Charles James Fox.* By J. Hancock,	53 mm		488	Æ	40
	251.4	*Earl St. Vincent's Reward.* By C. H. Küchler,	46 mm		489	Æ̷	400
	251.5	*Lord Nelson's Return to England.* By T. Halliday,	38 mm		490	Æ	40
						WM	25
	251.6	*Union of Ireland with Great Britain.* By J. Hancock,	38 mm		494	Æ	30
						WM	10
1801	252.1	*George III, Recovery from Illness.* By J. Hancock,	39 mm		503	Æ	40
						WM	10
	252.2	*Sir Ralph Abercromby.* By T. Webb (Mudie's medal).	41 mm		504	Æ	15
	252.3	*Admiral Lord Keith/Death of Abercromby.* By J. Hancock,	48 mm		507	Æ	60
						WM	30
	252.4	*Maj. General Hutchinson, Egypt Delivered.* By T. Webb (Mudie's medal).	41 mm		509	Æ	15
	252.5	*Battle of Copenhagen.* Unsigned,	38 mm		510	Æ	60
						WM	30

Date	No.		Pic	B.H.M.	Metal	Value
	252.6	*Sir Ralph Abercromby/London Highland Society.* By G. F. Pidgeon, 49 mm	*	512	Æℛ	120
					Æ	40
	252.7	*Preliminaries for Peace of Amiens.* By C. H. Küchler, 48 mm		513	Æℛ	150
	252.8	*Preliminaries for Peace of Amiens.* By H. Kettle, 38 mm		516	Æ	20
					WM	10
	252.9	*Preliminaries for Peace of Amiens.* Medallets. 17–25 mm		517–522	Æ	10
	252.10	*Union of Ireland with Great Britain.* By C. H. Küchler, 48 mm	*	523	Æℛ	150
					Æ	45
	252.11	*Union of Ireland with Great Britain.* By J. Hancock, 38 mm		526	Æ	25
					WM	10
	252.12	*Union of Ireland with Great Britain.* By P. Kempson, 48 mm		527	Æ	50
1802	253.1	*George III, Peace of Amiens.* By C. H. Küchler, 48 mm		534–536	Æ	50
	253.2	*George III, Peace of Amiens. Celebrations in St. Paul's Cathedral.* By J. Hancock, 49 mm	*	541	Æ	30
	253.3	*George III, Peace of Amiens. Marquis Cornwallis.* By J. Hancock, 39 mm		539	Æ	15
					WM	5
	253.4	*Death of Duke of Bedford.* By J. Hancock, 42 mm	*	532	Æ	20
1803	254.1	*Robert Banks, Secretary of State.* By J. Hancock, 50 mm		548	Æ	40
	254.2	*Barber Beaumont,* Duke of Cumberland's Sharpshooters. Unsigned. 41 mm	*	549	Æ	30
	254.3	*Boydell's Shakespeare,* published. By C. H. Küchler, 47 mm		553	Æℛ	55
	254.4	*Henry Addington,* Chancellor of the Exchequer. By J. Hancock and Kempson, 49 mm			Æ	15
1804	255.1	*William Betty,* Actor. (Young Roscius). By T. Webb 42 mm	*	557–558	Æ	30
					WM	10
	255.2	*William Betty,* Actor. By J. Westwood, 45 mm		559–560	Æ	35
					WM	10
	255.3	*Death of Joseph Priestley,* Chemist and theologian. By T. Halliday, 56 mm		563	Æ	70
					WM	25
	255.4	*E.I.C.'s Victory over French.* By J. P. Droz and G. Mills (Mudie's medal) 41 mm		567	Æ	15
1805	256.1	*George III, Visit to Weymouth.* Unsigned. 38 mm		569	WM	15
	256.2	*George Cooke,* Actor. By T. Webb, 54 mm		570	Æ	35
	256.3	*The Battle of Trafalgar,* Boulton's medal. By C. H. Küchler, 47 mm		584	Æℛ	250
					Æ	75
					WM	45
	256.4	*The Battle of Trafalgar,* Dr. Turton's medal. By T. Wyon, Sr., 44 mm	*	586	Æℛ	275
					Æ	150
	256.5	*The Battle of Trafalgar,* Death of Nelson. By P. Wyon, 51 mm		579	Æℛ	150
					WM	40
	256.6	*The Battle of Trafalgar,* Death of Nelson. By A. Abramson, 40 mm		574	Æℛ	150
					WM	40
	256.7	*The Battle of Trafalgar,* Death of Nelson. By T. Webb, 53 mm	*	577	Æℛ	200
					Æ	75

● There are a number of other medals commemorating the Battle and the death of Nelson and medals are found for the various anniversaries of the event.

Date	No.		Pic	B.H.M.	Metal	Value
	256.8	*The Battle of Trafalgar*, Admiral Collingwood. Unsigned. 38 mm	*	593	Æ	45
	256.9	*Admiral Sir Sydney Smith*. By T. Webb, 54 mm	*	573	Æ	40
	256.10	*George III, Christ Church, Birmingham*. By T. Webb, 42 mm		601 604— 605	Æ Æ WM	40 25 10
1806	257.1	*Death of William Pitt*. By T. Webb, 53 mm	*	610	Æ	40
	257.2	*Death of Charles James Fox*. By T. Webb, 54 mm	*	604— 605	Æ Æ	80 35
		● *B.H.M.* lists 7 further medals				
1807	258.1	*William Wilberforce*, Abolition of the Slave Trade. By T. Webb, 53 mm	*	627	Æ Æ	150 50
	258.2	*William Wilberforce*, Abolition of the Slave Trade. M.P. for York. Unsigned. 36 mm		626	WM	40
	258.3	*The Slave Trade Abolished*. By G. F. Pidgeon and J. Philip. ℞ Arabic inscription. 38 mm	*		Æ Æ	150 40
		● Often placed in the medallic series, but made as a token by Macauley and Babington for use in Sierra Leone.				
	258.4	*York Elections, Lord Milton*. Issued by E. Thomason. 35 and 40 mm			WM	35
	258.5	*Centenary of Union with Scotland*. By T. Wyon, 83 mm		628	Æ	500
		The Chesapeake Incident. No medal.				
1808	259.1	*Wellington*, Arrival of English Army in Peninsular. By Brenet (Mudie's medal). 41 mm		635	Æ	15
	259.2	*Battle of Vimiero*. By J. Barre and G. Mills (Mudie's medal). 41 mm	*	637	Æ	15
	259.3	*George, Prince of Wales*, foundation stone of Covent Garden Theatre. By P. Rouw, 91 mm	*	638	Æ	125
1809	260.1	*George III, Golden Jubilee*. By J. Barber (for Rundell, Bridge and Rundell). 70 mm		641	Æ Æ	450 75
	260.2	*George III, Golden Jubilee*. By T. Wyon, 42 mm		653	Æ WM	25 10
		● The Golden Jubilee of George III was celebrated in 1809, when he entered the 50th year of his reign, and in 1810, at the completion of the year. *B.H.M.* lists 15 further medals for 1809.				
	260.3	*Death of Matthew Boulton*. After P. Rouw, 46 mm		659	Æ	60
	260.4	*Death of Matthew Boulton*. By C. H. Küchler, 48 mm		661	Æ	60
		● A medal by G. Pidgeon (63 mm) was struck in 1819 on the 10th anniversary of Boulton's death.				
	260.5	*Death of Sir John Moore*, at Corunna. By G. Mills and J. A. Couriguer (Mudie's medal). 41 mm	*	666	Æ	15
	260.6	*Wellington, Passage of the Douro*. By N. Brenet and E. Dubois, 41 mm		671	Æ	15
	260.7	*Wellington, Battle of Talavera*. By G. Mills and Lafitte (Mudie's medal). 41 mm		673	Æ	20
	260.8	*Covent Garden Theatre*, 'Old Price' riots. Unsigned. 43 mm	*	675	Æ WM	35 15
1810	261.1	*George III, Golden Jubilee*. Unsigned. ℞ 'Frogmore'. 48 mm	*	686	Æ	30
	261.2	*George III, Golden Jubilee, Salisbury Celebrations*. By C. H. Küchler, 48 mm		684	Æ	35
		● *B.H.M.* lists a further six Jubilee medals.				

Date	No.			Pic	B.H.M.	Metal	Value
	261.3	*Sir Francis Burdett*, imprisoned. Unsigned.	48 mm		689	Æ WM	15 8
	261.4	*Wellington's Successes.* By T. Wyon,	50 mm		699	Æ	35
	261.5	*British Victories*, 1797–1809. By W. Mossop,	43 mm		700	Æ	30
1811	262.1	*George, Prince of Wales*, appointed Regent. By T. Wyon, 48 mm		*	706	Æ WM	30 10
	262.2	*George, Prince of Wales.* Unsigned.	38 mm		709	Æ WM	15 10
	262.3	*James Sadler*, Balloonist. By P. Wyon,	53 mm	*	712	Æ WM	150 50
	262.4	*Wellington, Lines of Torres Vedras.* By J. Petit and E. Dubois (Mudie's medal). 41 mm		*	713	Æ	15
	262.5	*Lord Beresford, Battle of Albuera.* By T. Webb and N. Brenet (Mudie's medal). 41 mm			718	Æ	15
	262.6	*Duke of Gloucester*, Chancellor of Cambridge University. 48 mm				WM	15
1812	263.1	*Spencer Perceval*, Assassinated. By W. Turnpenny (?), 49 mm			729	Æ WM	40 15
	263.2	*John Bellingham, Executed* (for Perceval's assassination). Unsigned. 40 mm			724	WM	20

● Bellingham, a bankrupt broker, shot Spencer Perceval, the British Prime Minister, as he entered the lobby of the House of Commons. He was hanged six days later.

	263.3	*Lord Hill, Battle of Almarez.* By G. Mills and Gayrard (Mudie's medal). 41 mm			727	Æ	15
	263.4	*Sir Thomas Picton, Battle of Badajoz.* By G. Mills (Mudie's medal). 41 mm			730	Æ	15
	263.5	*Battle of Salamanca.* By N. Brenet (Mudie's medal). 41 mm		*	735	Æ	15
	263.6	*Wellington, Madrid re-captured.* By T. and P. Wyon. 45 mm			737	Æ	35
	263.7	*Wellington, Indian (1803) and Peninsular Victories.* 49 mm		*	744	WM	15
	263.8	*Wellington, 'Vota Publica'.* By T. Webb,	53 mm	*	746	Æ	35
1813	264.1	*Wellington, Battle of Vitoria.* By G. Mills and Lefevre (Mudie's medal). 41 mm			756	Æ	15
	264.2	*Wellington, Battle of the Pyrenees.* By N. Brenet (Mudie's medal). 41 mm		*	760	Æ	15
	264.3	*Lord Lynedoch, Battle of San Sebastian.* By T. Webb and G. Mills (Mudie's medal). 41 mm			761	Æ	15
	264.4	*Wellington, Surrender of Pamplona.* By B. Brenet and J. Droz (Mudie's medal). 41 mm			765	Æ	15
	264.5	*Manchester Pitt Club.* By T. Wyon, 49 mm (often found glazed)		*	771	Æ	45

● In the 1813–1814 period a number of Pitt Clubs were established and 20 of these issued medals to members:

Blackburn
Blackburn Hundred   Northwich
Birmingham   Nottingham
Dudley   Rochdale
Leicester   Saddleworth
Liverpool   Sheffield
London   Stirling
Manchester   Suffolk
Menai   Sunderland
Northumberland and   Warrington
Newcastle-upon-Tyne   Wolverhampton

Date	No.		Pic	B.H.M.	Metal	Value
1814	265.1	*Betrothal of Princess Charlotte.* By T. Webb, 53 mm	*	778	Æ	30
		● To Prince William of Orange – it was broken off after six months.				
	265.2	*George III, Centenary of House of Brunswick.* By T. Wyon, 50 mm	*	779	AR	80
					Æ	40
	265.3	*Battle of Toulouse.* By N. Brenet (Mudie's medal). 41 mm	*	789	Æ	15
	265.4	*The Peace of Paris.* By T. Halliday, 48 mm		802	Æ	35
					WM	10
	265.5	*The Peace of Paris.* By W. Wyon, GRAND NATIONAL JUBILEE. 45 mm			AR	65
					Æ	15
	265.6	*The Peace of Paris, George, Prince Regent.* By J. Barber and T. Wyon, 69 mm	*	805	AR	300
					Æ	75
	265.7	*The Peace of Paris.* By T. Wyon, 57 mm	*	818	Æ	25
		● *B.H.M.* lists 43 medals commemorating the Victories, Defeat of Napoleon and Peace of Paris.				
	265.8	*The Peace of Paris, Peace ratified in U.S.A.* By J. Hancock, 46 mm		341	Æ	15
	265.9	*Alexander I of Russia,* visit to England. By T. Webb, 54 mm		848	Æ	40
	265.10	*Frederick of Prussia,* visit to England. By J. Westwood, 43 mm		852	Æ	40
	265.11	*Visit of Allied Sovereigns to England.* By J. Barre (Mudie's medal). 41 mm		854	Æ	15
	265.12	*George Walker, Apprentice Boys of Derry Club.* By W. Mossop, 41 mm		855	AR	40
					Æ	20
1815	266.1	*Benjamin West,* Picture purchased. By G. Mills, 41 mm		862	AR	40
					Æ	15
	266.2	*Benjamin West, President of the Royal Academy.* By G. Mills, 41 mm		865	Æ	15
	266.3	*British Army in Netherlands.* By A. Depaulis (Mudie's medal). 41 mm		867	Æ	15
	266.4	*Flight of Napoleon from Elba.* By N. Brenet and A. Depaulis (Mudie's medal). 41 mm	*	869	Æ	20
	266.5	*The Battle of Waterloo.* By B. Pistrucci, electrotype 135 mm	*	870	Æ	150
		● Issued c. 1850 (often in 2 separate halves) – a number of modern copies have been made from time to time, and are of less interest – and value.				
	266.6	*The Battle of Waterloo,* Wellington. By N. Brenet (Mudie's medal). 41 mm		871	AR	45
					Æ	15
	266.7	*The Battle of Waterloo, Wellington.* By W. Mossop, 66 mm		876	Æ	100
					WM	35
		● A number of other medals, counters and box medals record the event, and the first campaign medal – The Waterloo Medal – was issued shortly afterwards, to all ranks present at the battle.				
	266.8	*The Marquis of Anglesey.* The Charge of the British at Waterloo. By G. Mills and A. Depaulis (Mudie's medal). 41 mm		859	Æ	15
		Surrender of Napoleon. By T. Webb and N. Brenet (Mudie's medal). 41 mm	*	884	Æ	15
	266.10	*Treaties of Paris.* By G. Mills and N. Brenet (Mudie's medal). 41 mm		892	Æ	15
1816	267.1	*Marriage of Princess Charlotte,* to Leopold of Saxe-Coburg (later Leopold I, King of Belgium). By T. Halliday, 54 mm	*	907	AR	150
					Æ	35

Date	No.		Pic	B.H.M.	Metal	Value
	267.2	*Marriage of Princess Charlotte*, to Leopold of Saxe-Coburg. By T. Halliday and P. Kempson, 38 mm		906	WM	20
	267.3	*Daniel O'Connell*, Irish Patriot. By W. Mossop, 49 mm		914	Æ	40
	267.4	*George, Prince Regent, Bombardment of Algiers*. By T. Wyon, 50 mm		923	Æ	40
	267.5	*Sir Joseph Banks*. By T. and W. Wyon, 40 mm	*	911	Æℝ	50
		● Later used on Royal Horitcultural Society's medal.				
	267.6	*Thomas Leyland and the Liverpool Election.* 40 mm			Æℝ	80
					Æ	35
1817	268.1	*George III, Dedication Medal*, for Mudie's series of *National Medals*. By T. Webb and A. Depaulis, 41 mm		933	Æ	15
	268.2	*George III, 58th Anniversary of Reign*. By W. Wyon, Barton's medal 25 mm			Æ	100
	268.3	*George, Prince Regent*, preserved from assault. By T. Halliday, 39 mm		935	WM	20
	268.4	*Queen Charlotte, Visit to Bath*. By P. Kempson. 38 mm	*	934	Æ	40
	268.5	*The Death of Princess Charlotte*. By E. Avern, 50 mm	*	936	Æ	40
	268.6	*The Death of Princess Charlotte*. By T. Webb and G. Mills, 50 mm	*	940	Æℝ	100
					Æ	25
	268.7	*The Death of Princess Charlotte*. By Kempson & Son, 26 mm		944–945	Æ	4
	268.8	*The Death of Princess Charlotte*. Set of 4 medals, similar bust, ℞ Birth, Marriage, Death, or Obsequies. Each 22 mm		946	Æℝ	20
					Æ	10
					WM	6
		● Value increases if the complete set is found in its original case.				
	268.9	*John Philip Kemple*, retires from stage. By J. Warwick, 41 mm		1210	Æℝ	75
					Æ	35
		● Issued to guests at a 'Farewell' banquet, and usually named on the rim. It is possible that the Æ medals were issued in 1823, on his death.				
	268.10	*The Ionian Islands*. By A. Depaulis (Mudie's medal). 41 mm		958	Æℝ	150
					Æ	40
	268.11	*George, Prince Regent*, Opening of Waterloo Bridge. By T. Wyon, 27 mm	*	961	Æℝ	15
		● An allocation of silver had been made for the Waterloo medal, the first campaign medal for issue to all ranks; these medals were struck from the remaining silver.				
1818	269.1	*The Death of Queen Charlotte*. Unsigned. 39 mm		963	WM	15
	269.2	*The Death of Queen Charlotte*. Medallets. By T. Kettle, 25 mm		964	Æ	5
1819	270.1	*Birth of Princess Victoria*. Unsigned. 17 mm		975	Æ	—
	270.2	*The Death of James Watt*. By J. Marrian, 54 mm		982	Æ	50
	270.3	*The Death of James Watt*, Obsequies. Unsigned. 45 mm		984	Æ	25
	270.4	*Wellington, Governor of Plymouth*. By T. Webb, 55 mm	*	986	Æ	20
	270.5	*"Peterloo" Massacre* (Manchester Riots). Unsigned. 62 mm		989	WM	65
1820	271.1	*The Death of George III*. By C. H. Küchler, 48 mm	*	991	Æ	40
	271.2	*The Death of George III*. By Kempson (?), 48 mm		992	Æ	30
	271.3	*The Death of George III*. By T. Wyon, 40 mm		1001	Æ	30
					WM	10
	271.4	*The Death of George III*. Medallets. By Kettle, 25 mm		993–994	Æ	10

George IV
(29 January 1820–26 June 1830)
Born 12 August 1762, eldest son of George III

Married in 1795 to Princess Caroline of Brunswick, but parted after the birth of Princess Charlotte; Caroline's lifestyle caused numerous problems on her return to England after the Accession. The style of the late Georgian medals continued throughout his reign. There are a few pieces which are obvious highlights, but for the most part they are of good quality but unmemorable. Mudie and Thomason continued the mass-market sponsorship that Boulton had introduced some twenty years earlier.

Date	No.		Pic.	B.H.M.	Metal	Value
1820	271.5	*George IV*, Accession. By Rundell, Bridge & Rundell, 70 mm (*often gilt*)		1010	Æ	40
	271.6	*George IV*, Accession. By T. Webb, 55 mm	*	1013	Æ	40
	271.7	*Queen Caroline, Accession.* By G. Mills, 54 mm		1019	Æ	35
	271.8	*Queen Caroline, Return to England.* By P. Kempson, 41 mm		1021	Æ WM	15 15
	271.9	*Queen Caroline, Return to England.* By J. Westwood, 43 mm		1023	Æ WM	25 15
	271.10	*Queen Caroline, Trial* (on account of her conduct abroad). By A. Desboeufs (?), 82 mm		1026	Æ	60
	271.11	*Queen Caroline and Count Bergami.* By P. Kempson, 41 mm		1030	Æ	35
	271.12	*Queen Caroline, Withdrawal of the Divorce Bill.* By P. Kempson, 41 mm		1032	Æ	35
	271.13	*Queen Caroline, Withdrawal of the Divorce Bill.* By J. Westwood, 43 mm		1036, 1037	WM	15
	271.14	*Queen Caroline, Withdrawal of the Divorce Bill.* Unsigned. ℞ Crowned monogram. 32 mm		1068	Æ	30
	271.15	*Death of Benjamin West.* By G. Mills, 41 mm		1055	Æ	15
1821	272.1	*Coronation, Official Medal.* By B. Pistrucci, 35 mm (1060 specimens struck) (800 specimens struck)	*	1070	AV AR Æ	550 60 20
	272.2	*Coronation.* By T. Halliday and P. Kempson, 49 mm	*	1073	Æ WM	20 10
	272.3	*Coronation.* By J. Hancock, 46 mm		1077	AR Æ WM	60 20 10
	272.4	*Coronation.* By J. Hancock, 34 mm		1083	AR Æ WM	40 20 10
	272.5	*Coronation.* By Rundell, Bridge & Rundell, 70 mm		1088	Æ	40
	272.6	*Coronation.* By Rundell, Bridge & Rundell, 50 mm		1089, 1090	Æ	35
	272.7	*Coronation.* By T. Wells, 46 mm		1095, 1098	Æ WM	20 10
		● *B.H.M.* records 44 medals, etc. for the event.				
	272.8	*George IV, Visit to Hanover.* By J. Hancock, 46 and 34 mm		1114	Æ WM	20 10
	272.9	*George IV, Visit to Ireland.* By J. Hancock, 46 and 34 mm		1117	Æ WM	20 10
	272.10	*George IV, Visit to Ireland.* By J. Hancock (?), 46 mm		1120	Æ WM	25 10
	272.11	*George IV, Visit to Ireland.* By T. Halliday, 45 mm		1122	Æ WM	25 15

Date	No.		Pic.	B.H.M.	Metal	Value
	272.12	*George IV, Visit to Ireland.* By W. Mossop, 43 mm		1126–1128	Æ WM	50 20
	272.13	*George IV, Visit to Ireland.* By B. Wyon and G. Mills, 51 mm		1137	Æ	50
	272.14	*The Death of Queen Caroline.* By P. Kempson, 40 mm		1138, 1139	Æ WM	35 15
	272.15	*The Death of Queen Caroline.* Unsigned. 41 mm		1146	Æ	20
	272.16	*The Death of Queen Caroline.* Jettons. 27–25 mm		1150–1156	Æ	5
	272.17	*Lt. Gen. Lord Combermere, Victories in the Peninsular.* By B. Faulkner, 41 mm	*	1157	Æ WM	25 10
	272.18	*Charles Hutton,* Weighs the Globe. By B. and T. Wyon, 44 mm		1158	Æ	18
	272.19	*Neat and 'Gas' Hickman,* Boxing Match. Unsigned. 41mm		1159	WM	35
	272.20	*George IV, Installation as Knight of St. Patrick.* By I. Parkes, 45 mm		1173	Æ	45
1822	273.1	*George IV, Visit to Scotland.* By W. Bain, 45 mm		1178–1180	Æ	20
	273.2	*George IV, Visit to Scotland.* By B. R. Faulkner, 52 mm		1181–1182	Æ WM	20 10
	273.3	*George IV, Visit to Scotland.* Unsigned. ℞ St. Andrew. 46 mm		1189	Æ WM	20 10
	273.4	*George IV, Visit to Scotland.* Unsigned. ℞ Order of St. Andrew. 45 mm		1192	Æ Æ WM	40 20 10
	273.5	*George Canning, Foreign Secretary.* By W. Bain, 50 mm	*	1198	Æ Æ	50 20
1823	274.1	*George IV, Visit to Southampton.* By W. Wyon, 54 mm ● The visit did not, in fact, take place.		1205	Æ	50
	274.2	*William Wellesley-Pole,* Lord Maryborough, Master of the Mint. By B. Pistrucci, 51 mm		1211	Æ Æ	120 45
	274.3	*George IV, Brighton Pier completed.* By B. Wyon, 53 mm	*	1215	Æ Æ	120 40
	274.4	*John Rennie, Sheerness Docks opened.* By W. Bain, 64 mm	*	1219–1220	Æ WM	60 30
1824	275.1	*George IV, Laudatory medal* (Naval Aid to Greece). By B. Pistrucci, 60 mm	*		Æ Æ	250 75
	275.2	*Death of Lord Byron.* By J. Woodhouse, 39 mm		1222	Æ WM	30 20
	275.3	*Death of Lord Byron.* By A. J. Stothard, 64 mm	*	1231	Æ	75
	275.4	*Sir Walter Scott.* By W. Wyon, 53 mm	*	1238	Æ Æ	60 20
	275.5	*Plymouth Dockyard renamed Devonport.* By Ellis and Ramsey, 55 mm		1244	Æ	30
	275.6	*H.M.S.'s Adventure and Beagle.* Jetton. 26 mm			Æ	30
1825	276.1	*Frederick, Duke of York* (The York Club, Dublin). By I. Parkes, (Often with suspender) 36 mm		1248	Æ	50
	276.2	*Loss of the East Indiaman Kent.* By T. Halliday, 50 mm	*	1250	Æ	50
	276.3	*Sir Francis Chantrey* (Sculptor). By W. Bain, 50 mm		1249	Æ	40

Date	No.		Pic.	B.H.M.	Metal	Value
1826	277.1	*The Duke of York.*		1255	Æ	70
	277.2	*George Canning.* A. J. Stothard's 'Great Men'		1256	Æ	30
	277.3	*John Flaxman.* Series, each 62 mm:		1259	Æ	30
	277.4	*James Watt.*	*	1261	Æ	70
	277.5	*Sir Walter Scott.*	*	1260	Æ	30
	277.6	*Lt. Gen. Lord Combermere, Battle of Bhurtpoor.* By B. Faulkner, 41mm	*	1263	AR	60
					Æ	25
		(same obverse as 272–17)			WM	10
1827	278.1	*The Death of Frederick, Duke of York.* By I. Parkes, Often gilt 76 mm		1282	Æ	70
					Æ	
	278.2	*The Death of Frederick, Duke of York.* By B. Pistrucci, 60 mm	*	1283	Æ	50
	278.3	*The Death of Frederick, Duke of York.* By T. Ingram, 44 mm		1278	Æ	30
	278.4	*The Death of Frederick, Duke of York and Obsequies.* By T. Ingram, 25 mm		1293	Æ	15
		● A number of other items commemorate this event.				
	278.5	*William, Duke of Clarence,* Lord High Admiral. By J. Henning, Often gilt 66 mm	*	1296	AR	120
					Æ	70
	278.6	*The Death of George Canning.* By T. Halliday, 39 mm		1299	Æ	15
	278.7	*The Death of George Canning.* By A. J. Stothard. 277.2 reissued and redated. 62 mm		1303	Æ	30
	278.8	*Wellington, C-in-C British Army.* By J. Henning, 63 mm		1313	Æ	40
	278.9	*Gloucester and Berkeley Canal completed.* By T. Halliday, 45 mm		1316	Æ	40
					WM	20
1828	279.1	*Daniel O'Connell, elected M.P.* By I. Parkes, 50 mm		1324	Æ	50
	279.2	*Sir Francis Burdett, Catholic Emancipation.* Unsigned. 43 mm		1331	Æ	75
	279.3	*Test and Corporation Act repealed.* By S. Clint, 60 mm		1332	Æ	40
	279.4	*George IV, Patron of the Arts.* By T. Halliday, 42 mm		1333	Æ	25
	279.5	*George IV, Improvement in Coining.* By T. Halliday, 42 mm		1334	Æ	25
	279.6	*Windsor Castle, remodelling completed.* By A. J. Stothard, for Rundell Bridge and Rundell, 72 mm		1337	Æ	150
1829	280.1	*Daniel O'Connell, Catholic Emancipation.* By E. Thomason, 42 mm	*	1343	WM	20
	280.2	*Wellington, Catholic Emancipation.* By T. Webb, 55 mm		1345	Æ	40
	280.3	*York Minster,* choir destroyed by fire. By Hardy, 45 mm		1360–1362	Æ	25
					WM	10
1830	281.1	*The Death of George IV.* By A. J. Stothard, 62 mm		1363	Æ	30
	281.2	*The Death of George IV.* By E. Avern, 51 mm		1365	AR	75
					Æ	30
	281.3	*The Death of George IV.* By W. Bain, 35–45 mm		1367–1373	Æ	20
					WM	8
	281.4	*The Death of George IV.* By T. Halliday, 45 mm		1375	WM	5
	281.5	*The Death of George IV.* Unsigned. ℞ Windsor Castle. 51 mm	*	1391	Æ	30
					WM	12
		● In all *B.H.M.* lists 49 items covering the death and obsequies.				

William IV
(26 June 1830–20 June 1837)
Born 21 August 1765, 3rd son of George III, married in 1818 to Adelaide and died without legitimate issue.

The passing of the Reform Bill gave cause to many 'commercial' medallions, but the artistic output was not great. His request for a simple Coronation Ceremony proved popular, but still *B.H.M.* records 50 medals for the event.

Date	No.			Pic.	B.H.M.	Metal	Value
1830	281.6	*William IV, Accession.* Queen Adelaide's medal. By W. Wyon. Bust ℞ legend.	70 mm		1414	Æ	751
	281.7	*William IV, Accession.* By Thomason. Bust either side.	55 mm		1423	Æ / WM	40 / 15
	281.8	*William IV, Accession.* By T. Halliday. 4 varieties.	38–45 mm		1416–1419	WM	5–15
	281.9	*William IV, Accession.* Several other small medals and jettons exist.				Æ or WM	5–15
	281.10	*Earl Grey, Prime Minister.* Jetton.	22 mm		1442	Æ	3
	281.11	*Earl Grey, Prime Minister.* By T. Halliday,	38 mm		1454	WM	12
	281.12	*Liverpool and Manchester Railway, Opened.* By T. Halliday. ℞ Liverpool Station.	49 mm	*	1458	Æ / WM	50 / 25
	281.13	*Liverpool and Manchester Railway, Opened,* George Stephenson. By T. Halliday (?),	47 mm	*	1459	WM	15
		● These two medals are the earliest of the Railway medals struck in England, and form the start of a fascinating series. The following item is included because of its Railway affiliations.					
	281.14	*William Huskisson,* Statesman, Death. By S. Clint,	63 mm		1447	Æ	35
		● Huskisson was run over by a train at the opening of the Liverpool and Manchester Railway – the first railway casualty.					
	281.15	*The Middlesborough Branch; Stockton to Darlington Railway.* By J. W. James,	44 mm		1464	WM	30
	281.16	*H. Hunt, M.P. and the Preston Election.*	30 mm			Æ	35
1831	282.1	*Coronation.* The official medal. By W. Wyon. Busts of King and Queen. 33 mm (1000 specimens struck) (2,000 specimens struck) (1,000 specimens struck)		*	1475	AV / Æ / Æ	550 / 35 / 15
	282.2	*Coronation.* By W. Wyon for Rundell Bridge & Co., obverse as 281.6	70 mm		1476	Æ	75
	282.3	*Coronation.* By T. Halliday. 5 varieties.	38–45 mm		1478–1482	Æ / WM	20 / 15
	282.4	*Coronation.* By T. W. Ingram. 11 varieties.	35–55 mm		1483–1493	Æ / WM	15–30 / 5–15
		Many other small medals were issued to commemorate the Coronation.				Æ or WM	5–15

Date	No.		Pic.	B.H.M.	Metal	Value
	282.5	*The Reform Bill*, introduced to Parliament. By T. Halliday, 46 mm		1535	Æ	25
					WM	15
	282.6	*The Reform Bill*, introduced to Parliament. By T. Halliday, 39 mm		1538	WM	15
	282.7	*The Opening of London Bridge*, City of London Series. By B. Wyon. ℞ the bridge. 51 mm (700 specimens struck)	*	1544	Æ	35
	282.8	*The Opening of London Bridge*, City of London Series. Small medal. By B. Wyon, 27 mm		1545	Æ	40
	282.9	*The Opening of London Bridge*. Jetton. 29 mm		1548	Æ	5
	282.10	*Robert Raikes*, 50th Anniversary of Sunday Schools. By Ingram and Halliday. 9 varieties. 38–47 mm		1551–1559	WM	10
	282.11	*Izaak Pitman*, Inventor of Stenographic Sound Hand. By Allen and Moore. ℞ legend in shorthand, 45mm ● Presumably struck in the 1850s	*		WM	15
1832	283.1	*The Reform Bill Passed*, City of London Series. By B. Wyon. Britannia with scroll. 51 mm		1603	ÆR	65
					Æ	25
	283.2	*The Reform Bill, Thomas Attwood*. By T. Halliday, 41–44 mm		1562–1567	Æ	25
					WM	15
	283.3	*The Reform Bill, Earl Grey*. By J. Davis, 41–43 mm		1579–1583	WM	15
	283.4	*The Reform Bill*. By T. Halliday, 49–51 mm		1587–1590	WM	12
	283.5	*The Reform Bill*. By J. Davis. ℞ plan. 51 mm		1578	WM	12
	283.6	*The Reform Bill*. By T. W. Ingram, 45 mm ● A great number of other medals record the event or people connected with it.		1601	WM	12
	283.7	*English, Scottish and Irish Reform Bills*. By T. Halliday, 39 mm		1630	Æ	20
	283.8	*Jeremy Bentham*, founder of University College, London, Death. By T. Halliday, 32 mm		1568	Æ	30
	283.9	*Sir Walter Scott*, Death. By W. Bain and B. Faulkner. ℞ The Lady of the Lake. 50 mm		1576	ÆR	60
					Æ	35
	283.10	*The Royal Pavilion, Brighton*. By J. Langridge. Views of Building. 58 mm ● Probably issued at the same time as the Accession medal of Victoria (288.15).	*	1643	Æ	150
					WM	35
1833	284.1	*The Cholera Orphan School*, Bilston. By J. Ottley. Opened after the epidemic of 1832. 45 mm		1653	Æ	40
	284.2	*The Polish Association*. By T. Halliday. Issued by those opposed to Poland becoming part of the Russian Empire. 41 mm		1654	WM	20
	284.3	*The British Temperance Society*. By J. Davis, for 'Total Abstinence'. 38 mm		1657	WM	6
	284.4	*Temperance Society*. By T. Halliday, 45 mm ● Temperance Societies originated in the U.S.A. and many hundreds of medals were to be issued by various branches spread throughout the world.		1659	WM	10
1834	285.1	*The Abolition of Slavery in the British Empire*. By J. Davis, 36–51 mm	*	1665–	Æ	65
					WM	25

Date	No.		Pic.	B.H.M.	Metal	Value
	285.2	*The Abolition of Slavery in the British Empire.* By T. Halliday, 32–42 mm		1669, 1670, 1673	Æ WM	65 25
		● The anti-slavery movement gained widespread propaganda by the liberal distribution of such medals – 'A voice from Great Britain to America' – and the series is widely collected, good quality items now being very rare.				
	285.3	*Sir John Soane*, Testimonial medal. By W. Wyon. ℞ the Bank of England. 57 mm	*	1662	ℛ Æ	75 30
	285.4	*Wellington*, Chancellor of Cambridge University. 38 mm		1663	Æ	15
	285.5	*Wellington*, Chancellor of Cambridge University. 55 mm		1664	Æ	25
	285.6	*The City of London School.* By B. Wyon. City of London Series. 58 mm (350 Æ specimens struck)		1680	ℛ Æ	80 35
		● This medal was later adapted as a prize medal and is often found named – and as such has less commercial value.				
		The Houses of Parliament, destroyed by fire. No Medal.				
1835	286.1	*Daniel de Lisle Brock*, Bailiff of Guernsey. By T. Halliday. 51 mm		1684	Æ WM	35 20
	286.2	*The Corporation Reform Act.* 48 mm		1689	ℛ WM	45 15
	286.3	*Myles Coverdale*, Tercentenary of the first English Bible. By J. Davis and others. 36–44 mm		1691– 1697	ℛ Æ WM	30 15 5–15
	286.4	*Birmingham Cemetery and Chapel.* By J. Ottley, 44 mm	*		ℛ Æ WM	60 20 10
		● Cemeteries might seem an unusual subject for medals, but others are recorded; 1848–299.4 and 1850–301.6.				
1836	287.1	*Charles Green*, Aeronaut. Balloon flight from London to Weilburg. By W. J. Taylor, 42 mm		1704	ℛ Æ WM	120 40 25
	287.2	*Birmingham Grammar School*, bust of Edward VI, founder. By J. Carter, 52 mm		1709	Æ WM	20 10
	287.3	*Wesleyan Methodist Conference*, Birmingham. By J. Ottley, 46 mm		1714	ℛ Æ WM	65 30 15
	287.4	*Princess Victoria.* By W. Wyon, 36 mm			ℛ Æ	60 25
1837	288.1	*Princess Victoria, Majority.* By G. R. Collis. ℞ pyramid. 53 mm		1734	WM	15
	288.2	*Princess Victoria Majority.* By J. Ottley. ℞ legend. 51 mm		1743	Æ WM	35 12
	288.3	*Princess Victoria, Majority.* By J. Davis, T. Halliday, J. Ottley and others. 24–52 mm		1735– 1747	Æ WM	10– 35 10– 15
	288.4	*Birmingham Grammar School.* By T. Halliday. 63mm 48 mm 41 mm			Æ WM Æ Æ WM	40 12 20 12 5
	288.5	*Enlargement of Birmingham Town Hall.* By J. Davis. 51 mm	*	1754	Æ WM	20 8

Date	No.		Pic.	B.H.M.	Metal	Value
	288.6	*Sir Robert Peel*, Rector Glasgow University. By J. Ottley, 46 mm		1749	Æ	15
	288.7	*The Death of William IV*. By J. Barber, from a Coronation medal. 58 mm		1717	Æ Æ WM	150 35 10
	288.8	*The Death of William IV*. By T. Halliday, 35–45 mm		1718–1720	WM	10
	288.9	*The Death of William IV*. By T. Ingram, 35–41 mm		1721–1723	WM	10
	288.10	*The Death of William IV*. By T. Kettle, 22 mm ● Several other medals exist recording the death.		1724	Æ	6
	288.11	*Obsequies for William IV at Windsor*. By W. Bain, 46 mm		1731–1732	Æ WM	40 15
	288.12	*Obsequies for William IV at Windsor*. By T. Halliday, 45 mm		1733	WM	15

Victoria
(20 June 1837–22 January 1901)
Born 24 May 1819, daughter of Edward, Duke of Kent, and grand daughter to George III. Married in 1840 to Prince Albert of Saxe-Coburg and Gotha

The continued growth of expertise in mechanical manufacturing methods and the availability of cheap labour ensured a most prolific output of medals. They were produced, by some, as art objects and rewards for the encouragement of the arts (i.e. the City of London and the Art Union Series). Most Royal portrait medals throughout the reign were the work of a single family – the Wyon's – whose output, both for the mint and for themselves, was prodigious. The Golden Jubilee of 1887 lent itself to a whole mass of medals and this was repeated even more fervently a decade later for the Diamond Jubilee. It was this event that was to see the first major 'new' medal designed for, and issued by, the house of Spink.

Date	No.		Pic.	Metal	Value
1837	288.13	*Accession to the Throne*. By W. Wyon, two varieties. 36 mm		Æ Æ	110 50
	288.14	*Accession to the Throne*. By G. R. Collis. ℞ legend. 51 mm		Æ WM	25 10
	288.15	*Accession to the Throne, the Royal Pavilion, Brighton*. By Langridge, ℞ as 283.10. 57 mm		Æ	60
	288.16	*Visit to the City of London*, City of London series. By W. Wyon. 55 mm (350 specimens struck) ● This medal bears the famous diademed bust that was adopted for the Penny Black postage stamp, introduced in 1840; an event not, in turn, commemorated by any medal.	*	Æ Æ	120 40
	288.17	*Visit to the City of London*. By J. Barber, 61.5 mm		Æ WM	25 10
	288.18	*Liverpool Station*. By T. Halliday. 2 varieties. 48 mm		WM	25
1838	289.1	*Coronation*. The Official Medal. By B. Pistrucci. ℞ the Queen crowned. 37 mm (1,369 specimens struck) (2,209 specimens struck) (1,871 specimens struck)	*	 Æ Æ Æ	 500 40 25

Date	No.		Pic.	Metal	Value
	289.2	*Coronation.* Large decorative medal. By B. Pistrucci. 96 mm	*	Æ	150
	289.3	*Coronation.* By J. Davis, 65 mm		WM	15
	289.4	*Coronation.* Other medals. 22–45 mm		WM	5–15
		● The Coronation gave rise to a huge issue of medals mainly in copper and white metal, but including small brass jettons and even glazed paper examples with printed designs.			
	289.5	*London–Birmingham Railway.* The Euston Arch. By G. R. Collis. ℞ the names of the directors. 73.5 mm		Æ	75
	289.6	*Abolition of Negro Apprenticeship*, West Indies. By J. Davis, 51 mm	*	Æ	65
				WM	35
		39 mm		WM	25
1839	290.1	*Victoria, portrait medal.* By A. J. Stothard, 46 mm		Æ	40
	290.2	*Wellington,* Dover Banquet. By B. Wyon. ℞ Castle. 55 mm	*	Æ	15
	290.3	*John Wesley,* Centenary of Methodism. By B. Carter. ℞ Hall. 48 mm		Æ	20
				WM	5
	290.4	*Charles Wesley,* Centenary of Methodism. By B. Carter. ℞ legend. 48 mm		Æ	30
				WM	10
1840	291.1	*Victoria and Prince Albert,* Marriage (10 February). By B. Wyon. ℞ Felicity. 89 mm	*	Æ	80
	291.2	*Victoria and Prince Albert,* Marriage. By T. Halliday. ℞ the Ceremony. 54 mm		WM	10
	291.3	*Victoria and Prince Albert,* Marriage. By B. Wyon. Smaller. ℞ arms. 46 mm	*	ÆR	50
				Æ	20
		● As with the Coronation a large variety of medals and jettons exist.			
	291.4	*Victoria and Prince Albert,* Marriage. average large		WM	5–15
	291.5	*Victoria and Prince Albert,* Marriage. average small		WM	3–5
	291.6	*Birth of the Princess Royal.* By A. J. Stothard. ℞ legend. 40 mm		Æ	30
	291.7	*Birth of the Princess Royal.* By T. Halliday. ℞ Britannia. 45 and 39 mm		WM	10
	291.8	*Thomas Clarkson.* By J. Davis. ℞ negro slave. 52 mm		Æ	40
				WM	25
	291.9	*Newcastle upon Tyne and Carlisle Railway.* By W. Wyon, 50 mm		ÆR	150
1841	292.1	*Victoria.* By W. Wyon. ℞ CUDI JUSSIT. 45 mm		Æ	25
	292.2	*Princess Royal,* Christened. ℞ Britannia. 46 mm		WM	6
	292.3	*Birth of the Prince of Wales* (November 9). By J. Davis. 54 mm		WM	10
	292.4	*Treaty of London.* By J. B. Roth. Arms ℞ figures.		ÆR	75
	292.5	*Wellington.* By B. Pistrucci. ℞ ancient helmet. 60.5 mm	*	Æ	50
	292.6	*Lord John Russell.* By A. J. Stothard. ℞ Free Trade.		Æ	15
	292.7	*The 12 Conservative Members of Parliament for Shropshire.* By T. Halliday. ℞ ALL FRIENDS ROUND THE WREKIN. 59 mm		WM	15
1842	293.1	*Prince of Wales,* Christened. By J. Davis. ℞ the ceremony. 54 mm		WM	5
	293.2	*New Royal Exchange,* Laying of the first stone. By W. Wyon. 45 mm		Æ	40
	293.3	*New Royal Exchange.* By T. Halliday. ℞ view of building. 61 mm		Æ	35
				WM	10
		● A number of medals exist by Halliday, Davis and others.			
	293.4	*New Royal Exchange,* Prince Albert. By A. J. Stothard. ℞ the building. 44 mm		Æ	20

Date	No.		Pic.	Metal	Value
	293.5	*Visit to Scotland.* By B. Wyon (as marriage) ℞ ADVENTUI.			
		89 mm		Æ	100
	293.6	*Visit to Scotland.* By J. Davis. ℞ crowned thistles.		Æ	30
		54 mm and smaller varieties.			
	293.7	*Treaty of Nanking with China.* By J. Davis. ℞ Chinese delegation.		WM	20
		64 mm			
	293.8	*The New Houses of Parliament.* By J. Davis. ℞ view from the river.		WM	25
		64 mm			
		44 mm		WM	6
	293.9	*Mehemet Ali.* By A. J. Stothard. ℞ 'The Overland Route to India'.		Æ	15
		58 mm			

● It was Mehemet Ali, as Viceroy to Egypt, who had presented 'Cleopatra's Needle' to Britain in 1819, though it was not erected in London until 1878.

Date	No.		Pic.	Metal	Value
1842 & 1843	293.10	*Sir Isambard Marc Brunel,* Thames Tunnel. By W. J. Taylor and J. Davis. Many varieties.	*	Æ	10–25
		62.5 mm and smaller		WM	2–15
1843	294.1	*Visit to France and Belgium.* By T. Ottley. The arrival ℞ legend.		WM	5
		50 mm			

● Most medals relating to the visit were struck in either France or Belgium.

Date	No.		Pic.	Metal	Value
	294.2	*Launching of the S.S. Great Britain,* The first propeller-driven ship to cross the Atlantic. By Allen and Moore. ℞ the ship.	*	WM	15
		51 mm			
	294.3	*Launching of the S.S. Great Britain.* By Allen and Moore.			
		45 mm	*	WM	15
		35 mm		WM	5
	294.4	*Daniel O'Connell.* Repeal of the Union. By J. Davis. ℞ harp.		Æ	25
		38 mm			
	294.5	*Daniel O'Connell.* Repeal of the Union. Unsigned. 35 mm		Æ	20
	294.6	*Nelson's Column.* By J. Davis. ℞ the column. 43.5 mm		Æ	15
	294.7	*Nelson's Column.* By W. Railton. 44 mm		WM	10
	294.8	*Stonehenge and Old Sarum.* By F. T. Price. 54 mm		WM	25
1844	295.1	*Royal Exchange Opened.* Thomas Gresham. By W. Wyon. ℞ statue before building.		Ꞧ	90
		74 mm		Æ	30
	295.2	*Royal Exchange Opened.* By W. Wyon. ℞ three shields.	*	Ꞧ	25
		27 mm		Æ	12
	295.3	*Royal Exchange Opened.* By T. Halliday. ℞ Wellington statue.		WM	10
		61.5 mm			
	295.4	*Royal Exchange Opened.* By J. Davis. 60.5 mm		WM	10
	295.5	*Royal Exchange Opened.* By Allen and Moore. Double portrait.		Æ	12
		50.5 mm		WM	6
	295.6	*Royal Exchange Opened.* Small brass or white metal.			2–5

● Many other varieties exist.

Date	No.		Pic.	Metal	Value
	295.7	*Wellington,* Statue erected. By J. Davis. 51 mm		Æ	25
	295.8	*Wellington,* Statue erected. By Allen and Moore. 39 mm		WM	5
	295.9	*London Missionary Society,* Jubilee. By J. Davis. ℞ preaching.		Æ	10–25
		61 mm; 51 and 40 mm			
	295.10	*John Williams Missionary Ship.* By J. Davis. ℞ ship. 41 mm	*	WM	10
	295.11	*Chichester Cathedral.* By I. Barker. Fine view ℞ Chichester Cross.		Æ	40
		60 mm		WM	15

Date	No.		Pic.	Metal	Value
	295.12	Genl. Tom Thumb (C. S. Stratton). By Allen and Moore, 40 mm	*	WM	10
		● Charles Stratton was a midget, a man in perfect miniature, beautifully proportioned and only 24 inches high. He was brought to Europe by P. T. Barnum, the American showman and 'the Prince of humbugs'.			
1845	296.1	*Royal Visit to Ohrdruf.* By F. Helfricht. ℞ legend. 39 mm		Æ	25
	296.2	*Prince Albert.* By W. Wyon. Rev. St. George. 56 mm		Æ	20
	296.3	*William IV's Statue.* By Allen and Moore. 62 mm		WM	8
	296.4	*The Great Britain,* experimental voyage to the River Thames. 45 mm	*	WM	15
1846	297.1	*Royal Visit to Guernsey.* ℞ legend. 31 mm		WM	15
	297.2	*Liverpool Sailors Home.* By Allen and Moore. ℞ building. 45 mm		WM	5
	297.3	*Abolition of the Corn Laws.* By J. Davis. 2 varieties. ℞ Free Trade. 44 mm		WM	5
	297.4	*Abolition of the Corn Laws,* Anti-Corn Law League. By Allen and Moore. ℞ portraits. 51 mm		Æ	20
	297.5	*Abolition of the Corn Laws.* By W. J. Taylor. 54 mm		Æ	15
	297.6	*Abolition of the Corn Laws.* 45 mm		WM	5
	297.7	*Abolition of the Corn Laws,* Richard Cobden. By Allen and Moore. 39 mm	*	Æ	10
		Famine in Ireland. No Medal.			
1847	298.1	*Royal Visit to Cambridge.* By J. Davis. ℞ presentation. 51.5 mm		WM	12
	298.2	*Royal Visit to Cambridge.* Smaller varieties.		WM	5–10
	298.3	*Prince Albert,* Chancellor of Cambridge University. By G. G. Adams. ℞ legend. 58 mm		Æ	75
	298.4	*Prince Albert,* Chancellor of Cambridge University. By J. Peters (?). 44 mm		Æ	15
	298.5	*Birkenhead Docks,* Ship. ℞ details. 54 mm		WM	10
	298.6	*Daniel O'Connell,* death. ℞ tomb. 39 mm	*	Æ	15
	298.7	*New Houses of Parliament Opened.* By Ottley. ℞ 'Westminster N. E. View', 73 mm	*	WM	20
	298.8	*New Houses of Parliament Opened.* By H. Hyams. ℞ Royal Exchange. 61 mm		WM	15
	298.9	*New Houses of Parliament Opened.* By Allen and Moore. 51 mm		WM	12
	298.10	*New Houses of Parliament Opened.* By J. Davis. 44 mm		Æ	25
		● The Art Union issued a medal of Sir Charles Barry in 1862. The reverse shows his new buildings with the Victoria Tower.			
1847–1848	298.11	*The Factory Act and 10 Hours Bill.* By Green & Co. 39 mm		ÆR / Æ	40 / 20
1848	299.1	*Chinese Junk in the Thames.* By T. Halliday. Several varieties, obverses Mandarin or Junk. 45 mm	*	Æ / WM	40 / 10
	299.2	*Chinese Junk in the Thames.* Smaller varieties.		WM	5
	299.3	*Lord George Bentinck,* death. By B. Wyon. ℞ legend. 51 mm		Æ	20
	299.4	*Church of England and Cemetery, Birmingham.* By T. Halliday. 39 mm		WM	10

Date	No.		Pic.	Metal	Value
	299.5	*Plymouth Breakwater and Lighthouse completed.* By Allen and Moore. 55 mm		WM	10
		● Designed by Walker and Burgess, with William Stuart Superintendent Engineer for 37 years.			
	299.6	*William Wordsworth*, Portrait medal. By L. Wyon, 36 mm	*	Æ	20
1849	300.1	*Members of the House of Commons.* By Lauer. ℞ the names. 95 mm		Æ	85
		● See also 1894 345.4.			
	300.2	*Queen Adelaide*, Death. By Allen and Moore. 27 mm		WM	5
	300.3	*Newcastle, High Level Bridge*, view. ℞ details of Royal visit. 46 mm		Æ	15
	300.4	*New Coal Exchange.* By B. Wyon. City of London Series. ℞ interior view. (350 specimens struck) 89 mm	*	Æ	40
	300.5	*New Coal Exchange.* By Allen and Moore. 39 mm		Æ WM	20 5
		27 mm		WM	3
	300.6	*Royal Visit to Ireland.* By T. Halliday. ℞ harp. 45 mm		WM	6
	300.7	*Royal Visit to Ireland.* Varieties by other medallists in several sizes.		WM	2–10
1850	301.1	*Sir Robert Peel*, Death. By Allen and Moore. ℞ tomb. ℞ legend. 46 mm		Æ WM	15 8
		39 mm		WM	5
	301.2	*Sir Robert Peel*, Death. By T. R. Pinches. 45 mm		WM	10
	301.3	*The Prince of Wales*, 'Britain's Hope'. By Allen and Moore. 27 mm		WM	5
	301.4	*Robert Stephenson.* By L. C. Wyon. ℞ Britannia Tubular Bridge (Menai Straits). 58 mm		Æℝ Æ	100 40
	301.5	*Menai Suspension and Tubular Bridges.* Published by J. Aronson, Bangor. 66 mm	*	Æ WM	100 30
	301.6	*The Leicester Cemetery.* By T. Halliday. 40 mm		WM	10

The Great Exhibition of 1851
The 'World's Show in London', organised by Prince Albert, and exhibited in the building later called the Crystal Palace, was an event that caused great numbers of cheap souvenir medals to be struck, indeed the largest group depicting a single British building. Some medals were even struck in the building. Most of the medals are by Ottley or Allen and Moore.

Date	No.		Pic.	Metal	Value
1851	302.1	*The Great Exhibition of 1851*, Prince Albert. ℞ the building. 73 mm	*	WM	15
	302.2	*The Great Exhibition of 1851*, conjoined busts. ℞ the building. 51 mm	*	WM	5
	302.3	*The Great Exhibition of 1851.* Others in various sizes up to 42 mm		Æ or WM	2–8
		● Taylor, *The Architectural Medal*, describes 33 different medal designs.			
	302.4	*The Great Exhibition of 1851.* Prize medal. Conjoined busts. By W. Wyon. ℞ by J. Domard (Council). 90 mm		Æ	100
	302.5	*The Great Exhibition of 1851*, Prize medal. ℞ By L. C. Wyon. 77 mm	*	Æ	40
	302.6	*The Great Exhibition of 1851*, Prize medal, Prince Albert. ℞ FOR SERVICES. 48 mm		Æ	10

Date	No.		Pic.	Metal	Value
	302.7	*Royal Visit to Worsley Hall.* By Allen and Moore. ℞ barge on lake. 51 mm		Æ	20
	302.8	*Royal Visit to Manchester.* By Allen and Moore. ℞ procession. 50 mm		Æ WM	25 5
1852	303.1	*Duke of Wellington*, death. By G. G. Adams. ℞ Britannia. 58 mm	*	Æ WM	30 12
	303.2	*Duke of Wellington*, death. By Allen and Moore. ℞ flags.		WM	10
	303.3	*Duke of Wellington*, death. Others in various sizes.		WM	2–10
1853	304.1	*Royal Visit to Dublin Exhibition.* By W. Woodhouse. ℞ legend. 44 mm		WM	15
	304.2	*William Dargan*, Dublin Exhibition. By W. Woodhouse. ℞ the building. 44 mm		WM	15
	304.3	*Tasmania, the Cessation of Transportation.* 57 mm	*	Æ WM	250 50
1854	305.1	*The Crystal Palace*, Opened after its removal to Sydenham. By Pinches. ℞ the building. 63 mm		WM	12
	305.2	*The Crystal Palace.* 41 mm		WM	3
	305.3	*The Crystal Palace*, Sir Joseph Paxton. By L. C. Wyon. ℞ the building. 63 mm		WM	3
	305.4	*The Crystal Palace.* 41 mm and 51 mm		WM	6–10
	305.5	*The Holy Alliance* (England and France). ℞ English or French legend. 44 mm	*	Æ WM	15 3
	305.6	*Victoria and Napoleon III.* By L. Hart. ℞ trophies. 72 mm ● A number of other medals relating to the Alliance were struck in France and are not listed here.		Æ	15
	305.7	*Battle of Alma.* By Pinches. Battle scene. 41 mm		Æ WM	25 15
	305.8	*Battle of Alma.* By Pinches. Trophies, struck at Crystal Palace. 41 mm		WM	10
	305.9	*Battle of Balaklava.* By Pinches. Battle scene. 41 mm		Æ WM	25 10
	305.10	*Battle of Inkerman.* By Pinches. Battle scene. 41 mm	*	Æ	25
	305.11	*Florence Nightingale.* By Pinches. 41.5 mm	*	WM	20
	305.12	*The American Arctic Expedition* (Dr. Kane). By L. C. Wyon. 32 mm		Aʹ Aℝ	500 100
1855	306.1	*Visit of Napoleon III and Empress Eugenie.* By B. Wyon. City of London Series. (350 specimens struck) 76 mm		Æ	35
	306.2	*Visit of Napoleon III and Empress Eugenie.* By Pinches. 41 mm		Æ WM	15 3
	306.3	*Visit of Napoleon III and Empress Eugenie and return Royal visit to France.* By L. C. Wyon. Double portraits. 41 mm		Æ	20
	306.4	*Visit of Napoleon III and Empress Eugenie.* By Montagny. 53 mm		Æ	15
1855	306.5	*Visit of Victor Emmanuel II of Sardinia.* By B. Wyon. City of London Series. (350 specimens struck) 76 mm		Æ	35
	306.6	*Lord Raglan, Death at Sebastopol.* By J. Pinches. 41 mm	*	Æ WM	35 15
1856	307.1	*Peace to Europe and the Fall of Sebastopol.* 51.5 mm	*	WM	10
		The Victoria Cross instituted. No medal.			
1857	308.1	*The Sepoy Mutinies in India.* By Pinches. ℞ Victory with prisoner. 63 mm	*	WM	15

Date	No.		Pic.	Metal	Value
	308.2	*Art Treasures Exhibition, Manchester*. By Pinches. 63 mm		WM	8
		41 mm		WM	3
1858	309.1	*Marriage of the Princess Royal to Frederick William of Prussia*. By L. C. Wyon. Double Portrait. 63 mm	*	Æ	65
				Æ	25
	309.2	*Marriage of the Princess Royal to Frederick William of Prussia*. By Pinches. 41.5 mm		WM	5
	309.3	*Aston Hall*, Birmingham. By Ottley. 74 mm		Æ	40
				WM	15
	309.4	*Aston Hall*. Smaller. By Ottley. 55.5 mm		Æ	25
				WM	10
	309.5	*Opening of the Newport Dock*. By J. Moore. 57 mm		Æ	40
				WM	15
	309.6	*Victoria, Visit to Warwick Castle*. By J. Pinches. 42 mm		Æ	25
				WM	12
		Launching of S.S. Great Eastern. No medal.			
1859	310.1	*Isambard Kingdom Brunel*, Death. By J. Moore. ℞ The Great Eastern. 45 mm	*	Æ	25
				Æ	20
		36 mm		WM	10
	310.2	*The Great Eastern*, American medal. By J. Merriam, 31mm		WM	12
	310.3	*Robert Burns*, Centenary of birth. By J. Moore 43 mm	*	WM	5
1860	311.1	*The Great Eastern*. 31 mm		Æ	15
				WM	5
	311.2	*Scottish Volunteers*, Royal Review. By G. Dowler. 44 mm	*	WM	8
	311.3	*Prince of Wales, Visit to Canada*. By J. S. Wyon. 48 mm	*	Æ	40
				Æ	20
	311.4	*Royal Dramatic College*, Foundation Stone laid. By W. Brown, *always gilt* 24 mm	*	WM	10
1861	312.1	*Death of Prince Albert*. By J. Moore. ℞ Britannia weeps.		Æ	20
				WM	8
	312.2	*Prince of Wales, Visit to Ireland*. By I. C. Parkes, Medallet. 18.5 mm		Æ	6
	312.3	*The Great Eastern*. ℞ specifications, 'will carry 10,000 Troops", etc. 34 mm	*	WM	15
1862	313.1	*International Exhibition*. By Pinches. 51 mm		Æ	15
				WM	5
		● On the site of the present Natural History Museum, London.			
	313.2	*International Exhibition*. Smaller. By Pinches. 41.5 mm		WM	3
	313.3	*International Exhibition*. By J. Wiener. Prince Albert. ℞ 'stamped in building'. gilt or silvered base metal 41 mm	*	Æ	10
		A number of other medals were struck for the exhibition, some in memory of Prince Albert.		Æ or WM	3–15
	313.4	*International Exhibition*, Prize medal. By L. C. Wyon. 79 mm	*	Æ	18
	313.5	*Hartley Colliery Disaster*. By J. S. and A. B. Wyon. ℞ Symbolic rescue scene. 51 mm		Æ	25
1863	314.1	*Princess Alexandra in London*. By J. S. & A. B. Wyon. City of London Series. (350 specimens struck) 76 mm		Æ	35
	314.2	*Prince of Wales, Marriage to Princess Alexandra of Denmark*. By L. C. Wyon. Double portrait. 63 mm		Æ	85
				Æ	30
	314.3	*Prince of Wales, Marriage to Princess Alexandra of Denmark*. By Ottley. 51.5 mm	*	WM	5

Date	No.		Pic.	Metal	Value
	314.4	*Prince of Wales, Marriage to Princess Alexandra of Denmark*. A number of other medals were struck.		Æ or WM	3–10
	314.5	*The Nile Explored by Speke and Grant*. By J. S. and A. B. Wyon. 37 mm	*	WM	35
	314.6	*Blackpool Pier, opened.* 31 mm		WM	5
1864	315.1	*Shakespeare Tercentenary*. By L. C. Wyon. ℞ Shakespeare and the Centuries. 63.5 mm	*	Æ	40
	315.2	*Clifton Suspension Bridge*. By J. Moore. 46 mm	*	WM	10
1865	316.1	*Lord Palmerston*, Death. By W. Mack. 44.5 mm		WM	5
	316.2	*The Reform League*. By Maher and Son. 44 mm		WM	3
	316.3	*Richard Cobden*, Death. By E. Weigand. 41 mm		Æ	25
	316.4	*St. Patrick's Cathedral Dublin, Restored*. By W. T. Parkes. 65 mm	*	Æ	50
1866	317.1	*Royal Visit to Wolverhampton*, Prince Consort Statue. By Ottley. 65 mm		WM	10
	317.2	*Princess Helena, Marriage to Prince Christian of Schleswig Holstein*. By J. S. and A. B. Wyon. 64 mm	*	AR Æ	70 25
	317.3	*The Atlantic Submarine Telegraph Cable*. By J. Pinches. 26 mm	*	Æ	15

● Attempts to lay a telegraph cable in 1857 and 1858 both failed. A third attempt in 1858 was successful; on August 5th Queen Victoria telegraphed to the President of the United States, but the cable lasted only 3 months. The new cable was laid by the Great Eastern in July (having failed the previous year) and on the 30th of that month the Queen again telegraphed the President.

A much larger medal (79 mm) was made by J. S. and A. B. Wyon for the presentation by the American Chamber of Commerce, Liverpool.

Date	No.		Pic.	Metal	Value
1867	318.1	*The Federation of Canada*. By J. S. Wyon. 76 mm		AR Æ	500 100
	318.2	*The Reform Bill Passed*. By W. J. Taylor. 38 mm		WM	5
	318.3	*'Hermit', Derby Winner*. ℞ 'Run in a Snowstorm'. 33.5 mm	*	WM	10

● Derby Day was May 22nd. Hermit, owned by Mr H. Chaplin, was trained by Capt. Machell at Bloss's stable, Newmarket. He was ridden by J. Daley, and, in a sensational finish, won by a head. At 1000/15 his trainer won £3,000.

Date	No.		Pic.	Metal	Value
	318.4	*Abdul Aziz, Sultan of Turkey*, Visit to London. By J. S. and A. B. Wyon. City of London Series. (350 specimens struck) 76 mm		Æ	40
	318.5	*The Duke of Edinburgh*, Visit to Melbourne, Australia. By T. Stokes. 23mm		AV AR	200 60
1868	319.1	*The Prince of Wales, in Dublin*. By F. H. Mares. 51 mm		Æ	15
	319.2	*William Ewart Gladstone*, candidate for S. W. Lancashire. 44 mm		WM	10
	319.3	*The Duke of Edinburgh*, H.M.S. Galatea in Australia. By T. Stokes. 47 mm		WM	40
1868	319.4	*Giffard's Balloon, Captive Ascents*. By La Bouche. gilt 51 mm	*	WM	15

● The balloon *Captive* never got off the ground. Its replacement, in 1869, broke loose and finally crashed in Claydon Park. The medal, recording details of flights that never took place, is an interesting part of this financial failure.

Date	No.		Pic.	Metal	Value
1869	320.1	*The Holborn Viaduct and Blackfriars Bridge.* By G. G. Adams. City of London Series. (400 specimens struck) 76 mm		Æ	35
	320.2	*Thomas Graham, Master of the Mint,* Death. By J. W. Minton. 47 mm	*	Æ	20
1870	321.1	*Prince Albert; The Albert Memorial.* By J. S. and A. B. Wyon. 33 mm	*	Æ	15
		● The Memorial, an Eleanor Cross with a spire 150 feet high, was designed by Gilbert Scott. It was completed in 1872, but the statue by Foley was not finished and does not feature on this medal.			
1871	322.1	*Princess Louise, marriage to the Marquis of Lorne.* By J. S. Wyon. 64 mm	*	Æ	80
		Football, the F.A. Cup introduced. No medal.			
1872	323.1	*Prince of Wales, National Thanksgiving for his Recovery.* By J. S. and A. B. Wyon. City of London Series. (400 specimens struck) 76 mm		Æ	40
	323.2	*Prince of Wales, National Thanksgiving for his Recovery.* By J. S. Wyon. ℞ Plumes. 58 mm	*	Æ Æ	65 25
	323.3	*London Annual Exhibition of Fine Art.* By G. Morgan. ℞ Albert Hall. 70 mm gilt		WM	10
		● The medallist is best known for giving his name to his design for the U.S. silver dollar – the Morgan Dollar.			
	323.4	*London Annual Exhibition of Fine Art.* By J. S. and A. B. Wyon. Prince of Wales. ℞ Albert Hall. 30 mm		WM	4
1873	324.1	*London Annual Exhibition of Fine Art.* By J. S. and A. B. Wyon. Victoria. ℞ Albert Hall. 30 mm		WM	4
	324.2	*Visit of Naser-Ed-Din,* Shah of Persia. By A. B. Wyon. City of London Series. (400 specimens struck) 77 mm		Æ	40
	324.3	*Visit to Naser-Ed-Din,* Shah of Persia. Small medallets. 24 and 29 mm	*	Æ	5
	324.4	*London Annual Exhibition of Fine Art.* By G. Morgan. As 1872 medal. 70 mm	*	Æ	15
	324.5	*The Prince and Princess of Wales,* Bolton Town Hall opened. 39 mm		WM	10
1874	325.1	*Visit of Alexander II, Emperor of Russia.* By C. Wiener. City of London Series. (400 specimens struck) 77 mm		Æ	35
	325.2	*David Livingstone.* Royal Geographical Society medal. By A. B. Wyon. 37 mm		Æ	40
		● The medals are sometimes found named to the native bearers who carried Livingstone's body from Ilala to the coast. These medals have suspension loops, and are valued at a premium.			
	325.3	*The Tichborne Claimant.* By A. C. Darby. 42 mm	*	WM	12
	325.4	*Visit of the Fleet to Sunderland.* 30.5 mm		Æ	5
	325.5	*London Annual Exhibition of Fine Art.* By G. Morgan and E. Boehm, as 1872–1873. 51 mm		Æ	12
	325.6	*Duke of Edinburgh, Marriage to Princess Marie Alexandrowna of Russia.* By A. B. Wyon. 30 mm		Æ WM	10 6
	325.7	*Duke of Edinburgh, Marriage to Princess Marie Alexandrowna of Russia.* By C. Schnitzspahn (Darmstadt). Busts right. ℞ arms. 63 mm		Æ Æ	45 25
	325.8	*Prince and Princess of Wales,* visit to Ralph Heaton & Sons, The Mint, Birmingham. 37 mm		Æ	25

Date	No.		Pic.	Metal	Value
1875	326.1	The Alexandra Palace, opened, May Day, architectural view. 51.5 mm		WM	5
	326.2	S. Plimsoll. By A. Chevalier. ℞ 'Coffin Ship'. 35.5 mm and 26 mm	*	Æ	4
		● Plimsoll gave his name to the Plimsoll Line to prevent the over-loading of ships.			
	326.3	Daniel O'Connell, Centenary. By T. Parkes. 41.5 mm		Æ	15
	326.4	Thomas Carlyle. By G. Morgan and E. Boehm. 56 mm		ÆR	150
				Æ	50
		Capt. Matthew Webb. First to swim English Channel. No medal.			
1875–	326.6	Prince of Wales, Visit to India. By Phillips. Oval medal,	*	ÆR	75
1876		crown suspender, bust left. ℞ plumes.		WM	15
1876	327.1	Prince of Wales, return from India. 30.5 mm		WM	3
1877	328.1	Empress of India. By G. G. Adams. Crowned bust, legend on three scripts. 57 mm		Æ	40
		● More often found as the silver award, with suspender and ribbon.			
	328.2	Robert Burns, statue at Glasgow. By Gillespie Bros. mm		Æ	8
	328.3	Alfred the Great, Statue at Wantage. By W. J. Taylor. 35 mm	*	Æ	5
	328.4	Manchester Town Hall opened. By Pinches. 40 mm		WM	3
		First Lawn Tennis Championship, Wimbledon. No medal.			
1878	329.1	Temple Bar demolished. By C. H. and J. Mabbs for Foote Abbat. Made from lead removed from the roof. City of London Series. 102 mm		Pb	80
		● Often found in massive glazed frame with brass surround.			
	329.2	Nottingham Castle, Opened as Museum. 38 mm		WM	5
	329.3	'State Visit to Blackpool', by the Lord Mayor of London. 45 mm		WM	8
1879	330.1	Arthur, Duke of Connaught, Marriage to Princess Louise Margaret of Prussia. By J. S. and A. B. Wyon. Busts left. ℞ arms. 64 mm		ÆR	65
				Æ	30
	330.2	William Ewart Gladstone, Aged 70. By L. C. Wyon. 44 mm	*	ÆR	35
				Æ	15
	330.3	H.M.S.H. The Prince of Mantua and Montferrat. By Raddeley Bros. ℞ 508 persons cured . . . at Greenwich, etc. 54 mm		WM	10
1880	331.1	George I, King of Greece, Visit. By G. G. Adams. City of London Series. (400 specimens struck) 76 mm		Æ	40
	331.2	Benjamin Disraeli, Earl of Beaconsfield. By C. Dressler. 31 mm	*	Æ	5
	331.3	Gladstone and Marquis of Salisbury. By Oldacre & Co. 33 mm		Æ	5
	331.4	Robert Raikes, Sunday Schools Centenary. 33–44 mm		WM	2–5
1880	331.5	Charles Parnell, M.P., 'Home Rule'. 25 mm		Æ	3
	331.6	The Boycott Expedition. By West & Son. ℞ Loyal and Brave Ulsterman. Only 71 specimens issued. 39.5 mm	*	ÆR	250
		● Capt. Boycott refused to accept rents fixed by his tenants in Co. Mayo. As a result he was 'boycotted'.			
		The First Test Match. England and Australia at Cricket. No medal.			

Date	No.		Pic.	Metal	Value
1881	332.1	*International Medical Congress*. By J. Tenniel and L. C. Wyon. Sometimes silver medals are frosted and glazed. 77 mm		Æ Æ	55 30
	332.2	*Scottish Volunteers Anniversary*. By N. Macphail. Bust of Victoria. ℞ figures. 70 mm	*	Æ	25
	332.3	*Scottish Volunteers Anniversary, Review*. By D. O. Smith 44 mm 28 mm		Æ Æ	8 5
	332.4	*Benjamin Disraeli*. By J. Ottley. 44 mm		WM	8
	332.5	*Benjamin Disraeli, Death*. By C. Dressler. 35 mm		Æ	10
1882	333.1	*Royal Visit to Epping Forest*. By C. Wiener. City of London Series. (400 specimens struck) 77 mm		Æ	35
	333.2	*City of London School, opened by the Prince and Princess of Wales*. By J. S. and A. B. Wyon. City of London Series. (400 specimens struck) 77 mm		Æ	35
	333.3	*Leopold, Duke of Albany, marriage to Princess Helen of Waldeck*. By J. S. and A. B. Wyon. Busts right. ℞ arms. 64 mm		Æ Æ	65 30
	333.4	*Leopold, Duke of Albany, Visit to the Preston Guild*. By J. S. and A. B. Wyon. 51 mm		Æ	20
	333.5	*Royal Courts of Justice*, opened by Queen Victoria. 34 mm		WM	5
1883	334.1	*John Brown*. Private presentation medal from Queen Victoria. Bust left. 13 mm		N	—
	334.2	*Francis Drake, Statue at Tavistock*. By J. E. Boehm. 53 mm		Æ	25
	334.3	*Thomas Coats*, The Paisley Observatory. By N. Macphail. 49 mm		Æ	25
	334.4	*John Bright, M.P. for Birmingham*, since 1857. By J. Moore. 46 mm	*	WM	5
1884	335.1	*Sir Moses Montefiore*, Centenary. By A. D. Lowenstark. Hebrew legend around bust. 41 mm		Æ WM	15 5
	335.2	*New Council Chamber, Guildhall*. By J. S. and A. B. Wyon. City of London Series. (400 specimens struck) 76.5 mm		Æ	40
	335.3	*W. E. Gladstone*, Foundation Stone laid at the National Liberal Club. By Kenning. 77 mm	*	Æ	25
	335.4	*The New Reform Bill, passed*. By Maher & Son. 44 mm		WM	15
1885	336.1	*General Gordon*, the Latest Christian Martyr. By W. O. Lewis. Bust in fez. ℞ legend. 45.5 mm	*	WM	15
	336.2	*Princess Beatrice, marriage to Prince Henry of Battenberg*. By A. Wyon. Busts left. ℞ Arms. 64 mm		Æ Æ	65 35
	336.3	*Freedom of City presented to Prince Albert*. By G. G. Adams. City of London Series. (400 specimens struck) 77 mm		Æ	35
	336.4	*Centenary of The Times Newspaper*. By Strongi'th'arm. ℞ the clock. 44.5 mm	*	Æ	35
	336.5	*Alfred, Lord Tennyson*, Poet Laureate. By J. W. Minton (undated). Bust left. 47.5 mm		Æ	15
	336.6	*International Inventions Exhibition*. By L. C. Wyon. 45.5 mm		Æ Æ	25 10
	336.7	*Albert Palace, Battersea Gardens, London, opened*. 18 mm		WM	3
1886	337.1	*The Colonial and Indian Reception*. By Elkington & Co. City of London Series. (450 specimens struck) 77 mm		Æ	25
	337.2	*The Colonial and Indian Reception, Queen Victoria*, opening. 40 mm	*	Æ	30
	337.3	*The Colonial and Indian Reception, Prince of Wales*. By L. C. Wyon. 52 mm		Æ	6

Date	No.		Metal	Value
	337.4	*Liverpool International Exhibition.* By Elkington. 51 mm	Æ	5
	337.5	*Royal Visit to Liverpool.* 33.5 mm	WM	3
	337.6	*City of Ripon, Millenary.* 36 mm	Æ	8
	337.7	*The Great Eastern.* Visit to Dublin (as a floating exhibition palace), 33 mm	WM	15
1887	338.1	*The Golden Jubilee of Queen Victoria.* The official medal, by J. E. Boehm and Frederick, Lord Leighton *		
		(944 specimens struck) 58 mm	AV	1000
		(2,289 specimens struck) 78 mm	AR	80
			Æ	20
	338.2	*The Golden Jubilee of Queen Victoria.* By A. Scharff. City of London Series. (450 specimens struck) 77 mm	Æ	40
	338.3	*The Golden Jubilee of Queen Victoria.* By A. Gilbert. Art * Union Series. 64 mm	AR	250
			Æ	100
		● Issued as prizes 1887–1888 – 60 silver specimens and 80 bronze specimens.		
	338.4	*The Golden Jubilee of Queen Victoria.* By A. Wyon. 64 mm	Æ	35
	338.5	*The Golden Jubilee of Queen Victoria.* By J. Carter. 65 mm	Æ	35
	338.6	*The Golden Jubilee of Queen Victoria.* By J. Pinches. 36.5 mm	Æ	
	338.7	*The Golden Jubilee of Queen Victoria.* By J. Pinches (unsigned), for the India Rubber & Telegraph Works Co., Silvertown. Green, Brown & orange Bakelite 39 mm		10
	338.8	*The Golden Jubilee of Queen Victoria.* By T. Brock. ℞ The Imperial Institute. 38.5 mm	AR	15
		● The obverse makes use of Brock's rejected design for a new coinage portrait with a crowned and laureate bust to left.		
	338.9	*The Golden Jubilee of Queen Victoria.* Heaton Mint. Manchester Jubilee Exhibition. 45 mm *	Æ	10
			WM	3
	338.10	*The Golden Jubilee of Queen Victoria,* Royal Scottish Volunteers. By N. Macphail. 63 mm	Æ	25
			WM	10
		● The Golden Jubilee was a widely celebrated event. Many local boroughs issued medals (for dignitaries at receptions, schools, etc.), with common obverses and suitable reverses. The listing above shows a few of the types of a more general interest.		
		Collectors of local medals may well find some of the pieces hard to find; the cheapness of the manufacture placed them in a 'throw-away' class.		
1888	339.1	*Prince and Princess of Wales,* Silver Wedding. By H. Grueber. 34 mm	Æ	12
			WM	5
	339.2	*Spanish Armada,* Tercentenary. By J. Carter. 45 mm *	Æ	15
			WM	5
	339.3	*W. E. Gladstone,* National Liberal Federation, Birmingham. By J. Carter. 39 mm	Æ	15
1889	340.1	*700th Anniversary of the Mayoralty of the City of London.* By A. Kirkwood & Son. City of London Series. (450 specimens struck) 80 mm	Æ	35
	340.2	*Visit of the Kaiser to Spithead Naval Review.* By L. C. Lauer. * Bust left. ℞ ships. 60 mm	Æ	40
			WM	15
	340.3	*Mr. and Mrs. Gladstone,* Golden Wedding. By L. C. Lauer. 60 mm	WM	15
	340.4	*H.M.S. Calliope – Capt. H. C. Kane.* Presentation medal from the Marquis de Leuville. 33 mm	WM	15
		● Calliope was the only surviving ship, of thirteen, when a hurricane hit the Bay of Apia in Samoa.		

Date	No.		Metal	Value
1890	341.1	*Penny Postage Jubilee*, showing Mulready envelope. By L. C. Lauer. Issued by Spink & Son. 65 mm *	Æ Æ WM	100 40 20
		● Although not struck at the Spink factory it is believed that this medal is the first of a long and continuing series of commemorative pieces issued by our Company.		
	341.2	*Queen of Roumania at Llandudno*. By W. Mayer. 32 mm	Æ	12
	341.3	*H.M. Stanley, Emin Pasha Relief Expedition*. By E. Halle. Royal Geographical Society medal. 125 mm	Æ	300
	341.4	*Edinburgh International Exhibition, S. Lee Bapty*. By H. B. Sale. 42 mm	WM	10
1891	342.1	*Visit of Kaiser Wilhelm II of Prussia*. By Elkington & Co. City of London Series. (450 specimens struck) 80 mm	Æ	40
	342.2	*Visit of the Kaiser*, German Exhibition, Earls Court. By W. Mayer. 70 mm	Æ	20
	342.3	*H.M.S.'s Royal Sovereign and Royal Arthur, Launched*. By L. C. Lauer. 65 mm	Æ	80
	342.4	*Royal Naval Exhibition*. By A. E. Warner. 38 mm	Æ Æ WM Æ	12 6 3 35
	342.5	*Henry Irving*, Actor. By Lauer for J. Rochelle Thomas. * 60 mm	Al	25
	342.6	*Blackpool Tower*, Foundation Stone. 38 mm	WM	5
1892	343.1	*Ulster Unionist Convention*, Belfast. By Gibson & Co. (sometimes gilt) 38 mm	Æ Æ	20 8
	343.2	*Duke of Clarence*, Death. Medallet. 24 mm	Æ Æ	3 35
	343.3	*Alfred, Lord Tennyson*, Poet Laureate, Death. By Lauer for Rochelle Thomas. * 60 mm	Al	25
1893	344.1	*Duke and Duchess of York*, Marriage. By G. G. Adams. City of London Series. (400 specimens struck) 76 mm	Æ	40
	344.2	*Duke and Duchess of York*, Marriage. By Spink & Son. Cameo busts, 2 varieties. * 50.5 mm	Æ Æ	30 15
	344.3	*Duke and Duchess of York*, Marriage. By B. and A., and others, 5 varieties. 38 mm	WM	3
	344.4	*Visit of the King and Queen of Denmark*. By F. Bowcher. City of London Series. (450 specimens struck) 76 mm	Æ	40
	344.5	*Princess Marie of Edinburgh*, Marriage to Crown Prince Ferdinand of Roumania. By A. Scharff. 50.5 mm	Æ Æ	60 20
	344.6	*Winchester College*, 500th Anniversary. By G. Frampton. 76 mm	Æ Æ	55 15
1894	345.1	*Tower Bridge Opened*, by the Prince and Princess of Wales. By F. Bowcher. City of London Series. * (450 specimens struck) 76 mm	Æ	45
	345.2	*Tower Bridge Opened*, by the Prince and Princess of Wales. By A. Miesch. 36 mm	WM	5
	345.3	*Manchester Ship Canal, Opened*. Unsigned. 36 mm	WM	5
	345.4	*Mr. W. E. Gladstone*. By Lauer for J. Rochelle Thomas. ℞ names of M.P.'s. 95 mm	Æ Æ	200 85
		● See also the earlier medal, 1849 299.1.		
1895	346.1	*Four Generations of the Royal Family*. By H. Grueber. Hollow 39 mm	Al	15
	346.2	*T. H. Huxley*, Death. By F. Bowcher. 63 mm	Æ Æ	80 25

Date	No.		Pic.	Metal	Value
	346.3	*Gigantic Wheel, Earls Court.* By H. Grueber.		Al	10
		Hollow 39 mm			
		● The wheel was dismantled in 1907.			
	346.4	*The Challenger Expedition.* By J. Crichton. 77 mm	*	Æ	65
		● H.M.S. Challenger was commissioned for a prolonged cruise for ocean exploration, 1872–1876. The *'Challenger Report'* was issued in 50 volumes, 1880–1895, under the direction of Sir Wyville Thomson, and from 1882 onwards, Sir John Murray. The medal commemorates its completion.			
1896	347.1	*Four Generations of the Royal Family.* Penny-sized medal.		Æ	2
		32 mm			
1897	348.1	*The Diamond Jubilee of Queen Victoria.* The official medals, by T. Brock, Old and Young heads.	*		
		(3,725 specimens struck) large 56 mm		A⁄	850
		(19,498 specimens struck) small 21 mm		A⁄	95
		large 56 mm		Æ	25
		small 21 mm		Æ	5
		large 56 mm		Æ	10
		● The value of these medals is increased if they can be found in their original cases, and when both case and medal are in Mint condition.			
	348.2	*The Diamond Jubilee of Queen Victoria.* By Bowcher and Spink & Son. City of London Series.	*	Æ	40
		(500 specimens struck) 77 mm			
	348.3	*The Diamond Jubilee of Queen Victoria.* By F. Bowcher, for Spink & Son. large 76 mm		Æ	80
				Æ	25
				WM	15
		medium 51 mm		Æ	40
				Æ	15
				WM	6
		smaller 38 mm		Æ	25
				Æ	10
				WM	4
		smallest 22 mm		A⁄	150
				Æ	15
		● Spink issued vast numbers of medals for the Jubilee, honouring the Empire, Royal Family, Religious and Political leaders, etc. as well as striking medals for municipal use.			
	348.4	*The Diamond Jubilee of Queen Victoria.* By the Birmingham Mint (M.B.T.D.). 39 mm	*	Æ	15
				Æ	10
				WM	3–5
		● Found with various reverses.			
	348.5	*The Diamond Jubilee of Queen Victoria.* Four Generations of the Royal Family. By H. Grueber. As 347.1. 32 mm		Æ	2
	348.6	*The Diamond Jubilee of Queen Victoria.* White metal medals. By a large number of manufacturers and artists, usually 39–44 mm		WM	2–10
	348.7	*Nelson, H.M.S. Foudroyant,* wrecked at Blackpool. Issued by Fletcher. 38 mm		Æ	5
	348.8	*Gigantic Wheel, Earls Court.* Penny-sized medal. 32 mm		Æ	3
	348.9	*Typhoid Epidemic, Maidstone,* Lord Mayor's medal. By Mappin & Webb. 32 mm	*	Æ	30
	348.10	*The Blackwall Tunnel.* By F. Bowcher for Spink & Son. 76 mm		Æ	25
1898	349.1	*Penny Post Anniversary.* By F. Bowcher, for Spink.		Æ	40
		33 mm		Æ	20
	349.2	The Burrator Reservoir, Plymouth. 45 mm	*	WM	5

Date	No.		Pic.	Metal	Value
1899	350.1	*Victoria, Visit to Bristol.* By F. Bowcher. 39 mm		WM	5
	350.2	*S.S. Maine, 'The American Ladies Hospital Ship Fund'.* 45 mm	*	AR	35
				WM	15
	350.3	*Gigantic Wheel, Earls Court.* By Spink & Son (known for other years also (see 1895 and 1897) and not always signed). Penny-sized medal. 32 mm		Æ	3
1900	351.1	*Victoria, Visit to Ireland.* By Spink & Son. 39 mm	*	AR	25
				WM	5
	351.2	*Victoria, Visit to Ireland.* By Sale. 32.5 mm		WM	3
	351.3	*Victoria, 81st Birthday.* By Sale. R Baden Powell. 31 mm		WM	5
	351.4	*The Boer War.* By Spink & Son. 39 mm		WM	10
	351.5	*Baden-Powell,* Mafeking. By Spink & Son. 45 mm	*	AR	40
				Æ	75
		22 mm		AR	15
				Æ	4
	351.6	*Lord Roberts.* By Spink & Son. 45 mm	*	Æ	25
		22 mm		AR	15
				Æ	4
	351.7	*The National Commemorative Medal, 'The Absent Minded Beggar'. (often gilt)* By Spink & Son. 45 mm	*	AR	30
				Æ	15
				WM	6
		22 mm		AR	10
				Æ	5

● Sold for charities, in conjunction with the publishing of Rudyard Kipling's poem in the Daily Mail.

	351.8	*The City Imperial Volunteers,* return from the Boer War. City of London Series. By G. Frampton. (550 specimens struck) 76 mm		Æ	40
	351.9	*Transvaal Souvenir.* By Fenwick. 38 mm		WM	5
	351.10	*Siege of Peking, Defence of Legations.* By J. Taylor-Foot. R MENE, MENE, TEKEL, UPHARSIN-ICHABOD! 57 mm		Æ	65
	351.9	The Princess of Wales' Private Military Hospital. By Warrington & Co, 58 mm		AR	75

● The hospital, at The Gables, Surbiton, was maintained by a Mr and Mrs Alfred Cooper, as an adjunct to H.R.H.S. Hospital Ship, for the sick and wounded from South Africa.

1901	352.1	*Victoria, Death.* By Sale. 39 mm		WM	5
	352.2	*Victoria, Death.* By Lauer. 24 mm		WM	3

● After the enormous output of medals for the Jubilees of 1887 and 1897, Queen Victoria's death was not the subject for much commemoration.

HOUSE OF SAXE-COBURG AND GOTHA

Edward VII
(22 January 1901–6 May 1910)
Born 9 November 1841, eldest child of Queen Victoria, married in 1863 to Princess Alexandra of Denmark.

The (postponed) Coronation in 1902 gave us a great variety of medals, though the enthusiasm of the two Jubilees of Queen Victoria was not matched. The standard of the commercial medal was poor, and the short reign did not seem to produce many important events that merited a medallic commemoration. The progressive medallic art that had developed firstly on the continent and especially in France had by-passed England, but had found its way to America – the English medals remained traditional and dull. However, the medals produced by Frank Bowcher, often for Spink & Son, were competant, well-worked pieces, with good relief and original design.

Date	No.			Pic.	Metal	Value
1901	352.3	*Edward VII, Accession.*	39 mm		Al	3
	352.4	*South African Campaign.* By E. Fuchs.	70 mm		Æ	60
					Æ	25
			44 mm		Æ	25
	352.5	*South African Campaign.* By F. Bowcher, for Spink & Son. ℞ Lord Roberts on horseback.	109 mm	*	Æ	80
		First Trans-Atlantic Radio Transmission, by Marconi. *No Medal.*				
1902	353.1	*Coronation.* The Official Medal. By G. W. de Saulles. Busts either side		*		
		(861 specimens struck) large 56 mm			AV	850
		(2,728 specimens struck) small 31 mm			AV	120
		large 56 mm			Æ	30
		small 31 mm			Æ	7.50
		large 56 mm			Æ	10

● As with the 1897 official medals, value increases for cased medals in mint condition. Medals are found (both official and otherwise) with the dates 26 June and 9 August. The first date was cancelled because of the emergency appendix operation which the King underwent.

Date	No.			Pic.	Metal	Value
	353.2	*Coronation.* By F. Bowcher, for Spink & Son.	76 mm		Æ	75
					Æ	35
			46 mm		Æ	30
					Æ	15
			40 mm		Æ	20
					WM	3
			32 mm		WM	3
			22 mm		Æ	8
	353.3	*Coronation.* By G. Frampton for the Mint, Birmingham, conjoined busts left.	52 mm		Æ	12
			35 mm		Æ	5
			24 mm		Æ	3

Date	No.		Pic.	Metal	Value
	353.4	*Coronation.* By E. Fuchs, for Elkingtons, conjoined busts right. 64 mm		Æ̵R	45
				Æ	12
		38 mm		Æ̵R	15
				Æ	8
	353.5	*Coronation.* Souvenir medals by J. A. Restall and others, including many municipal issues. Approx. 38 mm		Æ	5–10
	353.6	*Visit to the City.* By Searle & Co. City of London Series. (300 specimens struck) 76 mm		Æ	50
	353.7	*Natural Gas First Used for Light Power*, Heathfield, Sussex. By R. Neal. 39 mm	*	Æ	12
1903	354.1	*Edward VII.* Visit to Ireland. By Spink & Son. 31–5 mm		Æ	15
	354.2	*Joseph Chamberlain*, Visit to South Africa. Issued by Joseph Fray. Facing bust. 51 mm		Æ̵R	20
				Æ	10
	354.3	*Joseph Chamberlain*, Visit to South Africa. By J. A. Restall. 39 mm		Æ	8
	354.4	*President Loubet*, Visit to England. By F. Bowcher for Spink & Son. 32 mm	*	Æ	10
		● The visit that established the Anglo-French 'Entente Cordiale'.			
1904	355.1	*Capt. R. Scott*, Antarctic Explorer. Royal Geographical Society medal. By G. Bayes. 71 mm		Æ̵R	75
	355.2	*Kingsway and Aldwych Tunnel.* By Spink & Son. 33 mm		WM	3
1905	356.1	*French and British Fleets.* Exchange of Courtesies. By Spink & Son. 45 mm	*	Æ	20
				WM	8
	356.2	*Nelson, Trafalgar Centenary.* Issued by Spink & Son. 32 mm		WM	5
	356.3	*Sir Henry Irving*, Actor, Death. By J.A. Restall. 45 mm		Æ	15
	356.4	*University of Sheffield.* By F. Bowcher, for Spink & Son. 40 mm		WM	5
1906	357.1	*Prince and Princess of Wales*, Visit to India. 38 mm		WM	5
	357.2	*Prince and Princess of Wales*, Visit to Rangoon. 38 mm		WM	5
	357.3	*Prince of Wales*, The Austrian Exhibition, London. Austrian medal by L. Hujer. 62 mm	*	Æ	25
	357.4	*Inter-Parliamentary Conference.* By A. Wyon. 50 mm		Æ	25
	357.5	*Joseph Chamberlain*, 30 years M.P. for Birmingham. By J. Fray, obv. as 354.2 51 mm		Æ	12
	357.6	*John Pinches*, Medallist, Death. Oval, 25 × 32 mm		Æ	15
1907	358.1	*Edward VII, Visit to Cardiff.* By Spiridion. 51 mm			15
	358.2	*700th Anniversary of the Foundation of Liverpool.* By C. J. Allen. Large 64 mm		Æ̵R	45
				Æ	15
		small 32 mm		Æ	8
				WM	2
	358.3	*Allan Wyon*, Medallist, Memorial. By A. G. Wyon. 44 mm		Æ	30
	358.4	*Balloon School, Royal Engineers, Farnborough.* By A. Fenwick. Dated 1901, from Coronation medal obverse (sometimes plated) 33 mm	*	Æ	15
		● The Balloon School was formed to match German development. The balloon on the reverse of the medal, the first British Military Airship, was named the 'Nulle Secundus' by the King in May, 1907. In October it flew successfully around St. Paul's Cathedral, but was destroyed after landing at Crystal Palace.			
	358.5	*Selby Abbey*, Nave re-opened after fire. 39 mm		Pb	10

Date	No.		Pic.	Metal	Value
	358.6	*West Highland Aluminium, Kinlochleven.* 39 mm		Al	6
	358.7	*Boy Scout Movement*, founded by Baden-Powell. *No medal.*			
1908	359.1	*Olympic Games in London.* By B. Mackennal and Vaughton. 51 mm	*	Æʀ	40
				Æ	20
				WM	12
	359.2	*Franco-British Exhibition, 'Entente Cordiale'.* By F. Bowcher. 45 mm		Æʀ	40
	359.3	*Linnean Society*, Darwin and Wallace. By F. Bowcher. 48 mm		Æʀ	35
				Æ	10
1909	360.1	*Visit of King Manuel of Portugal.* By F. Bowcher for Spink & Son. 76 mm	*	Æʀ	200
	360.2	*Sir Ernest Shackleton*, Explorer. Royal Geographical Society medal. By G. Bayes. 71 mm		Æʀ	75
	360.3	*Birmingham University, opened.* By G. Frampton, obverse as 353.3. 35 mm		WM	5
		Women's Suffrage. No medal.			
		● Engraved silver medals were issued 'FOR VALOUR', to those who participated in hunger strikes (22 mm, suspension loop and bar; green, white and purple ribbon).			
1910	361.1	*Daily Mail London to Manchester Air Race.* French plaquette, by L. Cariat. 46 × 65 mm		Æ	75
		● Won by L. Paulhan in 4 hours, 6 minutes.			
	361.2	*Edward VII, Death.* By Spink & Son. Obverse as 356.1, ℞ In Memoriam 76 mm		Æ	35
		45 mm	*	Æ	15
	361.3	*Edward VII, Death.* By H. Grueber. 39 mm		Al	8
	361.4	*Edward VII, Death.* By Sale, ℞ adapted from Victoria's medal, 352–1. 39 mm		WM	3
	361.5	*Edward VII, Death and Funeral.* By Fattorini Bros. 38 mm		Æʀ	15

HOUSE OF WINDSOR

(proclaimed 17 July 1917)

George V
(6 May 1910–20 January 1936)
Born 3 June 1865, the only surviving son of Edward VII, became heir on the death of his elder brother Albert Victor, Duke of Clarence, in 1892. Married 6 July 1983 to his brother's fiancee, Princess Victoria Maud (May) of Teck (Queen Mary).

The short period up to the beginning of the Great War saw a continuation of artistically dull medals. The medals of the War have a separate introduction, on page 86. The artistic styles developing in Europe begin to find their way into British medal design and the Royal Mint showed some innovative designs at the 1924 Wembley Exhibition. Percy Metcalfe was to be the champion of this new style. It was a reign where every artistic and well made medal seemed to be matched by a great number of the stereotype mass-produced items.

Date	No.			Pic.	Metal	Value
1910	361.6	*Atlantic Fleet,* Visit to Queenstown (Ireland). By J. F. O'Crowley.	31 mm		Æ	20
1911	362.1	*Coronation.* The Official Medal. By B. Mackennal		*		
			(225 specimens struck) large 51 mm		N	800
			(719 specimens struck) small 31 mm		N	120
			(2,117 specimens struck) large 51 mm		Æ	40
			small 31 mm		Æ	10
			large 51 mm		Æ	15
	362.2	*Coronation.* By F. Bowcher for Spink & Son.	109 mm	*	Æ	400
			64 mm		Æ	65
					Æ	25
			36 mm		Æ	20
					Æ	8
	362.3	*Coronation.* By J. Pinches. ℞ ship	39 mm		Æ	15
					Æ	8
	362.4	*Coronation.* By Vaughton. ℞ crown.	44.5 mm		Æ	12
	362.5	*Coronation.* By A. Toft, for The Birmingham Mint, ℞ ship.				
			35 mm		Æ	8
	362.6	*Investiture of Albert Edward as Prince of Wales.* By W. Gaspar John. (129 gold specimens struck) 31 mm		*	N	400
					Æ	30
	362.7	*The Delhi Durbar.* By F. Bowcher for Spink & Son. 64 mm			Æ	85
					Æ	25
			36 mm		Æ	25
					Æ	10
1912	363.1	*City of Oxford, Millenary.* By H. W. Page for Payne & Son. Modernistic City view. 57 mm		*	Æ	35
					Æ	15
					WM	6
	363.2	*National Aerial Campaign.* By P. Vaughton. 32 mm			Æ	15
	363.3	*Loss of S.S. Titanic.* Medal of Capt. A. H. Rostron of the rescue ship S.S. Carpathia. By T. Spicer Simpson. 51 mm			Æ	75
		● The Cunarder S.S. Carpathia was summoned by radio and rescued some 750 survivors – some of whom were later to sponsor this medal.				

Date	No.		Pic.	Metal	Value
1913	364.1	*Capt. R. Scott.* Royal Geographical Society medal. By F. Bowcher. 54 mm	*	Æ	50
	364.2	*H.M.S. New Zealand*, Maiden Voyage. By W. R. Bock. 36 mm	*	Ʀ	50

The medals of The Great War are widely collected but whilst the German Allies produced medals in vast numbers and the French and Belgiums did likewise, the British 'War Art' effort was directed elsewhere. The most common medal issued in this country was the one for the sinking of the S.S. Lusitania, and that was a copy of a German original, (1915, 366.3). Stories abound about this medal. The original, by Karl Goetz, was privately issued in Munich and mostly marketed through the firm of Jacques Schulman in Amsterdam (still very much coin dealers). The error in the date – May 5th not May 7th – was the fault of the Munich newspapers that reported the sinking with the incorrect date. Goetz repeated this mistake on his medal. The British took it to be proof positive that the medal demonstrated that the sinking was a premeditated plan of the most heinous nature. A French medal commemorates the British offensive of 1917 at Vimy, Arras and Ypres, but this piece, by S. E. Vernier and showing a Tommy advancing, was not issued until 1921.

Date	No.		Pic.	Metal	Value
1914	365.1	*George V*, Portrait Medal. By Huguenin. 50 mm		Ʀ	25
				Æ	10
	365.2	*Allied Heads of State.* 35 mm		Æ	4
	365.3	*Bombardment of Scarborough.* Issued by Spink & Son.		Ʀ	40
		32 mm	*	WM	10
		19 mm		Ʀ	10
	365.4	*Emmeline Pankhurst*, Votes for Women. 38 mm		Æ	5
	365.5	*New Zealand Division*, British Expeditionary Force. By Spink & Son. 45 mm		Ʀ	15
	365.6	*Royal Visit to Dundee.* 32 mm		Æ	4
1915	366.1	*Battle of Heligoland Bright and Doggar Bank.* By F. Bowcher for Spink & Son. 45 mm	*	Æ	15
				WM	10
		22.5 mm		A͞	75
				Ʀ	10
	366.2	*Anzac Landings in the Dardanelles.* By Dora Ohlfsen. 59 mm		Æ	35
	366.3	*Sinking of the S.S. Lusitania.* Copy of the German medal, issued for the Red Cross and St. Dunstans. 55 mm		Fe	5
		● This extremely common copy was issued for propaganda and little of the printed leaflet sold with it, in fact, is true. Boxed medals with the leaflet carry a small premium in value.			
	366.4	*Edith Cavell and Marie Depage.* Belgian medal by A. Bonnetain (struck 1919). ℞ REMEMBER. 62 mm	*	Æ	25
		● Nurse Cavell was shot by the Germans for being a spy. Marie Depage was a heroine on the S.S. Lusitania and went down with the ship.			
1916	367.1	*Lord Kitchener.* By Huguenin. 50 mm		Ʀ	30
	367.2	*Battle of Jutland.* By F. Bowcher for Spink & Son (to raise money for Naval Orphanages). 45 mm	*	Ʀ	15
				Æ	10
				WM	5
		22.5 mm		A͞	75
				Ʀ	10

Date	No.		Pic.	Metal	Value
	367.3	*Battle of Jutland.* By A. B. Pegram, for the Royal Numismatic Society. Lion over eagle. 76 mm		Æ Æ	75 30
	367.4	*Battle of Jutland.* By H. Stabler, for the Royal Numismatic Society. Ship Firing. 76 mm	*	Æ Æ	75 30
	367.5	*Battle of Jutland.* By W. Gilbert and C. Wheeler, for the Royal Numismatic Society. Admirals Jellicoe and Beatty. 76 mm		Æ Æ	75 30
	367.6	*German Prisoner of War Camp,* Douglas, Isle of Man. German medal (often in fitted wooden case). 45 mm ● Another, similar, was issued for the Camp at Knockaloe.		WM	35
	367.7	*Sir Roger Casement, Hanged for Treason.* German satirical medal, by K. Goetz. 57 mm	*	Fe	65
	367.8	*Shakespeare Tercentenary.* By D. Dicks. Facing bust. 51 mm		Æ Æ	35 15
1917	368.1	*David Lloyd George.* By F. Bowcher, for Spink & Son. 64 mm 45 mm	*	Æ Æ Æ	70 30 15
	368.2	*Lord Kitchener,* Death. By J. P. Legastelois. ℞ THOROUGH 45 mm 30 mm		Æ Æ	15 15
	368.3	*Mine Sweepers and Patrol Vessels.* By F. Gleichen. silvered 48 mm		Æ	30
	368.4	*Lord Roberts.* Workshop souvenir. silvered 26 mm		Æ	5
1918	369.1	*St. George's Day,* Zeebrugge and Ostend raids. By Spink & Son. 32 mm	*	WM	5
	369.2	*The Armistice* (the Cenotaph). By C. L. Doman. large 76 mm small 32 mm	* 	Æ Æ Æ Æ	45 20 20 10
	369.3	*Tyne Garrison,* 1914–1918. 41 mm		Æ	15
1919	370.1	*Peace.* By F. Bowcher for Spink & Son. 35 mm		Æ	8
	370.2	*Peace.* By The Birmingham Mint, 53 mm	*	Æ	10
	370.3	*Peace.* By Toye Kenning and Spencer. 39 mm		Æ	10
	370.4	Many municipalities and towns issued their own medals commemorating the Peace celebrations, mostly in bronze. Approx. 35 mm		Æ	5
	370.5	*The Sea Services Commemoration,* 1914–1919. 52 mm		Æ	12
1921	372.1	*Andrew Marvell,* Tercentenary. By T. Sheppard. 45 mm	*	Æ	15
1922	373.1	*The Prince of Wales,* International Boy Scouts Jamboree in Japan. Japanese medal. partial enamel on Æ 31 mm		Æ	25
	373.2	*The Prince of Wales,* Return from India. By F. Bowcher. ℞ Welcome Home. Oval 34 × 49 mm	*	Æ	50
	373.3	*H.R.H. Princess Mary,* Marriage. 26 mm		WM	2
		The B.B.C. commences broadcasting as station 2LO. *No medal.*			
1923	374.1	*William Harvey,* 800th Anniversary of St. Bartholomew's Hospital. By C. P. Jackson. 57 mm		Æ Æ	30 12
1924	375.1	*British Empire Exhibition.* Royal Mint souvenir medal (struck at the exhibition). 36 mm		Æ	10

Date	No.		Pic.	Metal	Value
	375.2	*British Empire Exhibition.* By P. Metcalfe. ℞ lion. 51 mm	*	Æ	15
1925	376.1	*The Prince of Wales*, Visit to Argentina. By J. M. Lubary. 50 mm		Æℝ	35
	376.2	*British Empire Exhibition.* By P. Metcalfe. ℞ three figures. 51 mm	*	Æ	15
	376.3	*The Prince of Wales*, visit to South Africa. By P. Metcalfe. 28 mm		WM	5
1926	377.1	*The Prince of Wales*, Empire Day. 39 mm		WM	3
	377.2	*The General Strike*, medal for services. By E. Gillick. 51 mm	*	Æ	15
1927	378.1	*University College*, London, Centenary. By P. Wilson Steer. 31.5 mm		Æℝ	25
1928	379.1	*Lloyds, New Buildings opened.* By F. Bowcher. 64 mm	*	Æ	20
	379.2	*Bert Hinkler*, Flight to Australia. By Stokes. 50 mm	*	Æ	20
	379.3	*Duke and Duchess of York.* (later George VI). Hospital opened at Weston-super-Mare. 33 mm		Æ	6
1930	381.1	*Opening of Liverpool Cathedral.* By E. Carter Preston. Modernistic plaque. 38 × 72 mm	*	Æ	35
1931	382.1	*Visit of King Faud of Egypt.* By P. Metcalfe and C. L. Doman. 76 mm	*	Æ	35
	382.2	*Marshall Street Baths*, in Westminster, opened, 38 mm	*	Æ	10
1933	384.1	*The First Flight over Mt. Everest.* By P. Metcalfe. 45 mm		Æℝ	200
	384.2	*Falkland Islands Centenary.* By B. Mackennal for the Royal Mint. 36 mm	*	Æ	35
1934	385.1	*The Duke of Kent*, Marriage to Princess Marina of Greece. By V. Phalireas. 68 mm		Æ	25
	385.2	*Cunard Liner '534'* (later S.S. Queen Mary – see 387.1). Daily Record medal. 32 mm	*	WM	3
	385.3	*The Mersey Tunnel*, opened by George V and Queen Mary. By Fattorini. 32 mm		Al	6
1935	386.1	*George V, the Silver Jubilee.* The Official Medal. By P. Metcalfe. large 58 mm	*	Æ⁄	850
				Æℝ	35
		small 32 mm		Æ⁄	120
				Æℝ	15
	386.2	*George V, the Silver Jubilee.* By Spink & Son. ℞ 'Modern' facing Britannia. 45 mm		Æ	15
	386.3	*George V, the Silver Jubilee.* Several varieties issued by municipalities and towns, etc. Approx. 22–38 mm		WM	2–10
1936	387.1	*Cunard Liner*, S.S. Queen Mary, Maiden Voyage. By G. Bayes. 70 mm	*	Æ	35
	387.2	*George V, Death.* 'The Best, The Gentlest and the Most Beloved'. 39 mm		Al	5

Edward VIII
(20 January–10 December 1936)
Born 23 June 1894, proclaimed Prince of Wales in July 1911. His abdication followed after a reign of almost 11 months and he married the divorced Mrs. Wallis Simpson, 3 June 1937. He died 28 May 1972.

The single year did not give time for any artistic developments, though 'souvenir' Coronation medals were struck by many companies and are still very plentiful today.

Date	No.			Pic.	Metal	Value
1936	387.4	*Proposed Coronation.* ℞ Britannia.	44.5 mm		Æ	10
	387.5	*Proposed Coronation.* By Spink & Son (low relief).	32 mm		AV	120
					AR	15
					Æ	5
	387.6	*Proposed Coronation.* By V. B.	38 mm		Æ	10
	387.7	*Abdication.* By L. E. Pinches. Crowned bust. ℞ legend in wreath.	35 mm	*	AV	500
					AR	30
					Æ	15
	387.8	*Abdication.* Large round Bakelite plaque with postage stamp and impressed with abdication speech. Issued by B. A. Seaby.	115 mm			25

George VI
(10 December 1936–6 February 1952)
Born 14 December 1895, second son of George V. Married 26 April 1923 to Lady Elizabeth Bowes-Lyon (the Queen Mother).

A fine double portrait Coronation medal by P. Metcalfe was the last official medal of that series. The Second World War produced no medals of merit and the post war revival in sport (1948, The Olympics) and industry and the arts (1951, The Festival of Britain), also failed to produce any original medal designs.

Date	No.			Pic.	Metal	Value
1936	387.9	*The Three Kings of 1936.* By J. Pinches. Issued in a set, George V, Edward VIII and George VI (sometimes silvered)				
			each 51 mm		Æ	30
			each 32 mm	*	Æ	15
		● Small premium on cased set in perfect condition.				
1937	388.1	*Coronation.* The Official Medal. By P. Metcalfe.				
		(274 specimens struck) large 58 mm			AV	1200
					AR	35
		(422 specimens struck) small 32 mm		*	AV	200
					AR	15
					Æ	5
	388.2	*Coronation.* Birmingham manufacture. Conjoined busts (several reverses).	35 mm		AR	25
					Æ	5
1938	389.1	*Neville Chamberlain,* Return from Munich – 'Peace in our time'. By M. Hiley.	62 mm		Æ	25
	389.2	*Neville Chamberlain,* Return from Munich. By V. Demanet. Uniface.	70 mm		Æ	40

Date	No.		Pic.	Metal	Value
	389.3	*Neville Chamberlain*, Return from Munich. Unsigned. 35 mm		Æ	25
	389.4	*Joseph Herman Hertz*, Chief Rabbi. By Benno Elkan 34 mm		Æ	20
	389.5	*London and Birmingham Railway*, Centenary. By J. Pinches. 65 mm		Æ	15
	389.6	*Star Newspaper*, Jubilee. 34 mm		Æ	8
1939		*Declaration of War. No medal.*			
1940		*The 1940 Club* (see 1959)			
1941	392.1	*Winston S. Churchill*, Prime Minister. Uniface plaque. By F. Kormis (and Spink & Son). 127 mm		Æ	65
		● Issued with the publication of *Mr. Churchill: An Intimate Portrait*. By Philip Guedalla.			
	392.2	*The Atlantic Charter*. By C. Magrath. 76 mm		Æ	—
		● Only four original specimens believed struck, however, a so-called 'limited edition' in gold, of the reverse, was issued in 1965. The value of that relates to the prevailing gold price.			
1943	394.1	Field Marshal Bernard Montgomery, Alamein, Tripoli and Tunis – 8th Army. By M. Fox, Cairo. 27 mm		A/	150
1944	395.1	*Battle of London*, 1940–1941 and 1944. By the Goldsmiths and Silversmiths Co. for the R.A.F Benevolent Fund. silvered 57 mm	*	Æ	25
1945	396.1	*Winston Churchill*, The Allied Victory. By A. Loewental. ℞ torch. 63 mm		Æ	20
	396.2	*Winston Churchill*, The Liberation of France. By P. Turin (French Mint, Paris). 68 mm		Æ	25
		● Restrikes still available.			
1946	397.1	*Victory Celebrations*. City of Westminster. 32 mm		WM	5
	397.2	*The Liberation of Jersey* (9 May, 1945). 'Cheap' souvenir medal. 35 mm		Æ	15
1947	398.1	*H.R.H. Princess Elizabeth*, Marriage to 'Lieut. Philip'. 34 mm		WM	5
	398.2	*Earl Mountbatten of Burma, Viceroy of India*. Uniface plaque. By F. Kormis. 140 mm	*	Æ	75
		● Issued 1948.			
1948	399.1	*The Olymic Games*, London. By J. Pinches, the B. Mackennal design of 1908 (359.1). 51 mm	*	Æ	15
		Birth of Prince Charles (14 November). *No medal.*			
1951	402.1	*The Festival of Britain*. 'Cheap' souvenir medal. 39 mm	*	Æ	5
		● Officially commemorated by a proof Crown (5-shilling piece).			
1952		*George VI, Death. No medal.*			

Elizabeth II
(6 February 1952–   )
Born 21 April 1926. Married 20 November 1947 to Philip Mountbatten, Duke of Edinburgh.

Sadly, there was no official medal to commemorate the Coronation and the official and other medals of the reign have been lacking in any great display of New Elizabethan art. The modern machinery prohibits, rather than encourages, the striking of high-relief medals and the expenses involved have done little to encourage patrons. A boom in precious metal prices in the 1960s saw the birth of a huge medal industry selling often inferior designs to a public eager to buy collectable gold and silver. The Krugerrand was yet to be accepted as a means of dealing in bullion. 1982 saw the birth of the British Art Medal Society; perhaps now we can look forward to better medallic designs with more certainty, and hope for more encouragement for the very existence of the medal as a 'Mirror of History'.

Date	No.			Pic.	Metal	Value
1953	404.1	*Coronation.* By Spink & Son. ℞ Buckingham Palace				
			large 57 mm	*	AV	—
					AR	40
					Æ	15
			small 32 mm		AV	120
					AR	20
					Æ	5
	404.2	*Coronation.* By H. Dropsy (Paris). ℞ Windsor Castle.			Æ	15
			50 mm			
	404.3	*Coronation.* By Fey. ℞ Britannia.	76 mm silvered		Æ	25
	404.4	*Coronation.* By The Birmingham Mint, ℞ the 1911 design by A. Toft.	37 mm		Æ	5
	404.5	*Coronation Royal Film Performance.*	35 mm	*	AR	30
		● The film shown was 'Rob Roy', starring Richard Todd and Glynis Johns.				
	404.6	*Coronation.* Other unofficial or municipal issues. By Fatorini, etc.	28–38 mm		Æ etc.	5–15
		● No official medals were issued (ending a tradition that started with the Coronation of James I), but a proof coinage was struck to commemorate the event.				
1953– **1954**	404.7	*The Royal Visit* (tour of the Commonwealth). By M. Gillick, for the Royal Mint.	39 mm	*	Æ	20
1954	405.1	*Winston Churchill*, 80th Birthday. By The Birmingham Mint (for the Conservative Association).	37 mm	*	Æ	10
1955	406.1	*Winston Churchill*, Retirement from the Premiership. By The Birmingham Mint (for the Conservative Association).	37 mm		Æ	10
	406.2	*150th Anniversary of Trafalgar.* By P. Vincze for Spink & Son.				
			large 57 mm		AV	—
					AR	40
					Æ	15
			small 32 mm		AV	120
					AR	20
					Æ	8
1958	409.1	*Sir Vivian Fuchs, Trans-Antarctic Expedition*, 1955–1958. By F. Kovacs. Royal Geographical Society medal. 65 mm		*	AR	40
1959	410.1	*Winston Churchill*, 85th Birthday, Presentation medal of the 1940 Club (Lord Beaverbrook's Ministry of Aircraft Production). By Spink & Son.	57 mm		AV	500

Date	No.		Pic.	Metal	Value
	410.2	*Wolfe and Montcalm; Canada, 1759–1959.* By P. Vincze for Spink & Son.		Æ	—
				Æ	40
		58 mm		Æ	15
1962	413.1	*Elizabeth II*, Poetry medal. By G. T. and E. Dulac for the Royal Mint. 55 mm gilt		Æ	35
1964	415.1	*Winston Churchill*, 90th Birthday. By R. Schmidt and C. Ironside. Both struck by the Austrian mint, Vienna, issued singly and in sets. 50 mm		Æ	—
		32 mm		Æ	200
		20 mm		Æ	100
1965	416.1	*Winston Churchill*, Death. By F. Kovaks for Spink & Son. ℞ 'Very Well Alone', after a cartoon by Low. 56 mm	*	Æ	—
				Æ	35
		39 mm		Æ	400
				Æ	20
	416.2	*Winston Churchill*, Death. By A. Loewental for B. A. Seaby, a re-issue of the 1945 medal. 50 mm		Æ	—
				Æ	30
				Æ	10

● The combination of public sentiment and the laws governing the sale of gold made Churchill's death the cause for a large output of gold medals, starting a trend that is still current today. The prices of these modern medals fluctuate with the price of bullion, and for this reason no prices are quoted on large gold medals.

The fact that some of these medals were probably never fully subscribed, together with the fact that the rise in the price of the gold has seen them sold for their melt value, has left many of them now genuinely scarce items.

Date	No.		Pic.	Metal	Value
	416.3	*Battle of Waterloo Reception.* 150th Anniversary at the Guildhall, London. City of London Series. 44 mm		Æ	12
	416.4	*400th Anniversary of the Royal Charter to Sark.* 20–30 mm		Æ	—
	416.5	*900th Anniversary of Westminster Abbey.* By M. Rizzello for the Royal Mint. (900 gold specimens struck) 58 mm		Æ	—
				Æ	30
				Æ	10
	416.6	*Ian Smith*, Rhodesia's Unilateral Declaration of Independence. 39 mm		Æ	15
				Æ	10
		24 mm		Æ	8
1966	417.1	*Ireland's Golden Jubilee.* By P. Vincze. 51 mm		Æ	—
				Æ	35
		38 mm		Æ	—
				Æ	15
	417.2	*England's World Cup (Football) Triumph.* By Superieties Ltd. gold plated base metal 29 mm		Æ	10
	417.3	*Prince Philip, Visit to North America.* By Spink & Son. (1,000 specimens struck) 31 mm		Æ	30

● 3 additional specimens were struck in Platinum.

Date	No.		Pic.	Metal	Value
	417.4	*900th Anniversary of the Battle of Hastings.* By Spink & Son. 58 mm		Æ	—
				Æ	30
		40 mm		Æ	—
				Æ	20

Date	No.		Pic.	Metal	Value
1967	418.1	*Sir Francis Chichester.* Single Handed Circumnavigation of the World. By P. Vincze for Spink & Son. 57 mm		Pt	—
				A/	—
				Æ	40
		38 mm		Pt	—
				A/	—
				Æ	20
	418.2	*Queen Elizabeth, The Queen Mother.* By C. Ironside struck at the Royal Mint for the National Trust. 39mm	*	Æ	20
1968	419.1	*R.M.S. Queen Elizabeth II,* Maiden Voyage. By L. G. Colley for Slade Hampton & Son. 65 mm		Æ	45
	419.2	*Jim Clark* (racing car driver) memorial. By M. Rizello. 57 mm		Æ	20
1969	420.1	*Installation of Charles, Prince of Wales.* Official medal. By M. Rizzello (Royal Mint). ℞ Welsh dragon.	*		
		(1,500 silver specimens struck) 57 mm		Æ	30
		gilt		Æ	15
		32 mm		Æ	18
				Æ	8
	420.2	*Installation of Charles, Prince of Wales.* By J. Pinches.			
		57 mm		Æ	30
		45 mm		Æ	20
		32 mm		Æ	10
	420.3	*Installation of Charles, Prince of Wales.* By Fey. ℞ arms. 52 mm		Æ	20
1970	421.1	*The S.S. Great Britain* Returns to Bristol. (see 1843, 294.2). 39 mm	*	Æ	8
	421.2	*Hudson's Bay Company,* Tercentenary. Canadian medal by Dora de Pedery Hunt, issued to shareholders. ● The Company's head office was then still in London.	*	Æ	5
	421.3	*350th Anniversary of the Mayflower and the Pilgrim Fathers.* By P. Vincze for Spink & Son.			
		57 mm		Pt	—
				A/	—
				Æ	35
		38 mm		Pt	—
				A/	—
				Æ	15
1971	422.1	*50th Anniversary of the First Northern Ireland Parliament.* By T. H. Paget and C. Ironside for the Royal Mint. 45 mm		Æ	35
		(5,000 silver specimens struck) 32 mm		Æ	10
1972	423.1	*Elizabeth II, Silver Wedding.* By M. and F. Feuchtwanger.			
		60, 50, 32 mm		A/	—
		25 mm		A/	65
		20 mm		A/	35
	423.2	*Royal Visit to Brunei,* Sultan Hassanal Bolkiah. By Spink & Son. 60 mm	*	Æ	75
				WM	15
	423.3	*TutanKhamun Exhibition* (British Museum). By D. F. Payne. 57 mm		Æ	15
	423.4	*H.R.H. The Duke of Windsor (Edward VIII),* Death. Issued by Coincraft (1984), 45 mm		Ni	8
				Æ	8
1973	424.1	*New London Bridge Opened, by the Queen.* By D. F. Payne. City of London Series			
		(2,250 Æ gilt specimens struck) 51 mm			
				Æ	30
				Æ	15

Date	No.		Pic.	Metal	Value
	424.2	*Lord Mais*, Lord Mayor of London. By D. F. Payne. 51 mm		Æ	15
	424.3	*Royal Mint, Queens Award for Industry*. Small 'dumpy' medal. 25 mm		Ꭱ	30
	424.4	*Sheffield Assay Office Bi-Centenary*. The Mints, Birmingham and London. gilt 51 mm		Ꭱ	25
		Britain Joins the Common Market (E.E.C.). *No medal.*			
1974	425.1	*General Election*. By the Mint, Birmingham. 45 mm		Ν	—
				Ꭱ	20
				Æ	10
1974	425.2	*J. B. Priestley*, author, 80th Birthday. By P. Vincze. 57 mm		Ν	—
				Ꭱ	35
	425.3	*Chinese Exhibition*, Royal Academy. By D. F. Payne. 51 mm		Æ	15
	425.4	*900th Anniversary of Robert the Bruce*. By Spink & Son for the National Trust of Scotland. 58 mm		Ν	—
				Ꭱ	30
				Æ	10
1975	426.1	*Common Market Referendum*. By the Mint, Birmingham. 38 mm		Ꭱ	25
				Æ	10
	426.2	*North Sea Oil*, The Forties Field, innaugurated by the Queen. Issued by B.P. 58 mm		Ꭱ	50
	426.3	*North Sea Oil*, The Argyle Field. By the Danbury mint. 45 mm		Ꭱ	25
		● Sold with a phial of oil supplied by Texaco.			
	426.4	*The Royal Mint*. The Closure at Tower Hill (before the removal to Llantrisant, S. Wales). By R. Elderton. 50 mm		Ꭱ	40
				Æ	15
	426.4	*H.M. Yacht Britannia*, 21st Anniversary. By Spink & Son. 38 mm (500 specimens struck)		Ꭱ	40
		● This medal, and subsequent Britannia medals (1977, 428.6; 1978, 429.2; 1984, 435.1), are issued numbered; the number 1 medal in each case being presented to H.M. The Queen.			
	426.6	*Eamon de Valera*, Irish Statesman, Death. By Spink & Son. 58 mm	*	Pt	—
				Ꭱ	30
		40 mm		Pt	—
				Ꭱ	20
1976	427.1	*Royal Visit to U.S.A.*, for Bicentenary of American Independence. By L. Lindsay for the Birmingham Mint. 32 mm		Ꭱ	20
	427.2	*Concorde*. First passenger flight, London–Bahrain. By Pobjoy mint. 40 mm	*	Pt	—
				Ꭱ	20
	427.3	*World of Islam Festival*. 46 mm		Ꭱ	20
1977	428.1	*The Silver Jubilee*. The official medal by the Royal Mint.			
	428.2	*The Silver Jubilee*. By L. Durbin for Spink & Son. Ꭱ Rose. 57 mm	*	Pt	—
				Ν	—
				Ꭱ	35
	428.3	*The Silver Jubilee*. By A. Machin, bust of H.M. The Queen, in high relief, a handsome medal to commemorate the celebrations in Washington, D.C., U.S.A. 60 mm	*	Ꭱ	60
	428.4	*The Silver Jubilee*. By the Birmingham Mint and other private issuers, approx. 38–45 mm		Ꭱ	20–30
		other metals			3–10
	428.5	*Sir Robin Gillett*, Lord Mayor of London in Jubilee Year. 39 mm		Ꭱ	30

Date	No.		Pic.	Metal	Value
	428.6	*H.M. Yacht Britannia*, Queen's Jubilee medal. By Spink & Son. (300 specimens struck) 38 mm		Æ	50
	428.7	*Wimbledon, Tennis Championship Centenary*. By Garrard. 44 mm		Pt AV Æ	— — 25
	428.8	*Charlie Chaplin*, film pioneer, Death. By K. Rolfson. 45 mm		Pt AV Æ Æ	— — 30 10
	428.9	*Pompei Exhibition* (Royal Academy). By Toye, Kenning and Spencer. 51 mm		Æ	25
1978	429.1	*75th Anniversary of the British Numismatic Society.* 77 mm		Æ Æ	75 25
	429.2	*H.M. Yacht Britannia*, 25th Anniversary. By Spink & Son. 38 mm (400 specimens struck)		Æ	45
1979	430.1	*Royal Visit to Malawi*, President Kamuzu Banda. By Spink & Son. 60 mm	*	Æ	75
	430.2	*European Elections* (to the European Parliament) By the Birmingham Mint. 40 mm		Æ	15
	430.3	*Margaret Thatcher, first Lady Prime Minister*. By the Birmingham Mint. 45 mm		Pt Æ Æ	— 20 10
1980	431.1	*Queen Elizabeth, The Queen Mother*, 80th Birthday. By L. Durbin for Spink & Son. 57 mm	*	AV Æ Æ	— 30 12
		38 mm		AV Æ Æ	— 20 8
	431.2	*City of Exeter*, 1900th Anniversary. By D. Holland and D. Andrews. 39 mm		Æ	10
	431.3	*Golden Hinde*. 400th Anniversary. By D. Holland and D. Andrews. 39 mm		Æ	10
	431.4	*Golden Hinde and Plymouth Festival.* 44 mm		Æ	6
1981	432.1	*Prince Charles, Marriage to Lady Diana Spencer*. By M. Rizzello for Spink & Son. 57 mm	*	AV Æ Æ	— 35 15
		38 mm		AV Æ Æ	— 20 10
	432.2	*Natural History Museum, London*, Centenary. silvered 45 mm		Æ	10
1982	433.1	*Falkland Islands Liberation.* silvered 38 mm	*	Æ	8
	433.2	*Pope John Paul II, Visit to Britain*. By P. Nathan for Spink & Son. 57 mm		AV Æ Æ	— 50 18
	433.3	*700th Anniversary of the Trial of the Pyx*. Replica trial plate. By the Royal Mint. Approx. 42 × 55 mm ● Given to guests at a luncheon held at Goldsmiths Hall.		Æ	50
	433.4	*The British Art Medal Society*. Inauguration 'Sheep Moor II'. By R. Dutton. 78 mm		Æ	35
		Birth of Prince William, of Wales. No medal.			

Date	No.		Pic.	Metal	Value
1983	434.1	*Margaret Thatcher*, Prime Minister's visit to the Falkland Islands. By P. Nathan for Spink & Son. 57mm	*	N	—
				R	50
				Æ	20
		38 mm		N	—
				R	30
				Æ	10
	434.2	*Royal Maundy Service*, Exeter. By the Tower Mint. (500 specimens struck) 44 mm		R	30
1984	435.1	*H.M. Yacht Britannia*. 30th Anniversary. By Spink & Son. (300 specimens struck) 38 mm	*	R	60
	435.2	*The Thames Barrier*. By R. Maclouf, for the Tower Mint, conjoined busts of H.M. The Queen and Prince Philip. (200 specimens struck) 39 mm	*	R	35
		(10,000 specimens struck)		CuNi	5

● A souvenir medal has also been struck for visitors to the Barrier.

The Illustrations

1.1

1.2

3.3

15.2

8.1

15.1

22.1

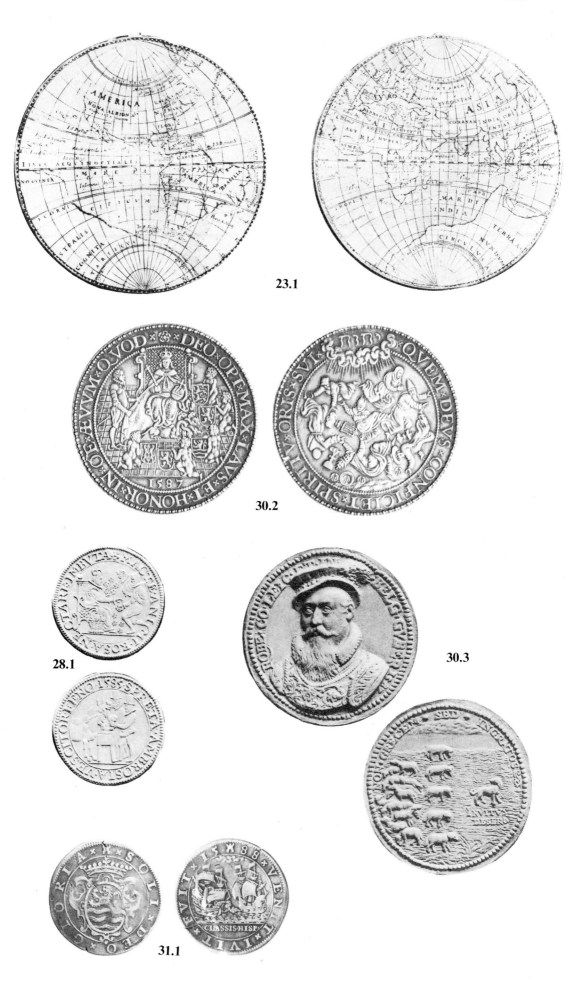

23.1

30.2

28.1

30.3

31.1

31.2

31.4

32.1

33.1

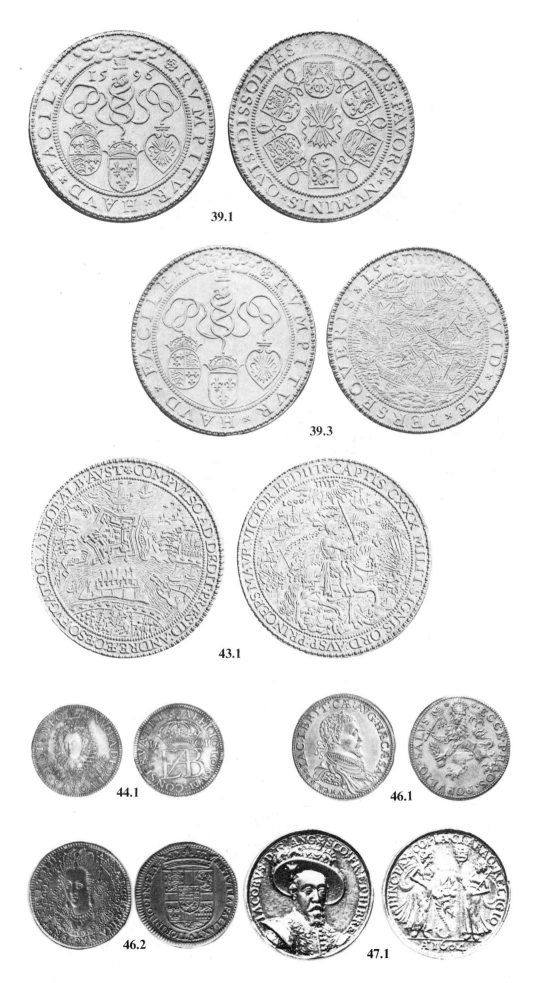

39.1

39.3

43.1

44.1

46.1

46.2

47.1

48.1

52.3

55.1

56.1

59.1

59.2

62.2

62.3

62.4

68.1

69.1

70.1

71.1

72.1

73.1

73.4

75.1

76.1

76.2

78.1

79.1

80.1

81.1

81.1

81.2

82.1

82.3

84.1

85.2

85.3

86.4

86.6

87.1

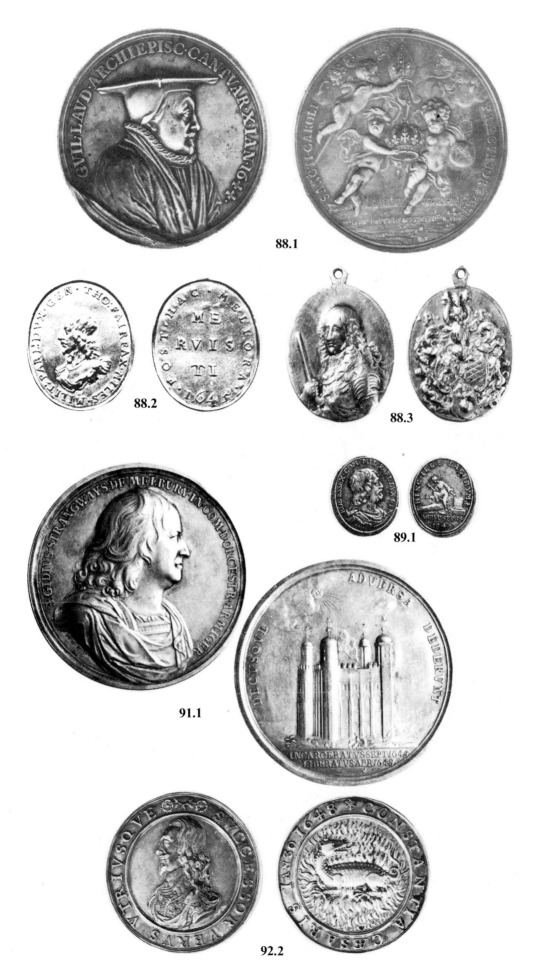

88.1

88.2

88.3

89.1

91.1

92.2

92.3

92.5

92.8

94.4

93.1

93.2

93.2
(variety)

93.1
(variety)

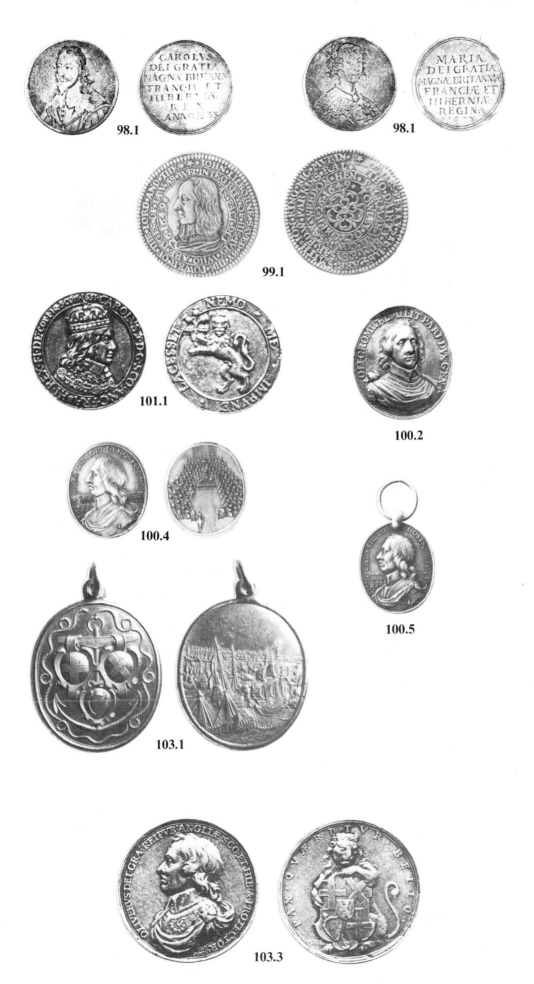

98.1

98.1

99.1

101.1

100.2

100.4

100.5

103.1

103.3

104.1

108.3

108.4

108.5

110.1

111.1

110

111.2

111.3

111.4

111

112.1

113.1

113.2

116.2

113.3

113.4

116.3

117.1

112

118.2

118.3

117.4

119.1

120.1

121.1

113

122.1

122.2

123.1

114

124.1

125.1

128.1

129.2

129.3

131.1

132.1

133.1

133.2

134.2

134.5

136.1

136.3

136.5

136.9

136.10

138.1

138.1

139.1

139.5

139.9

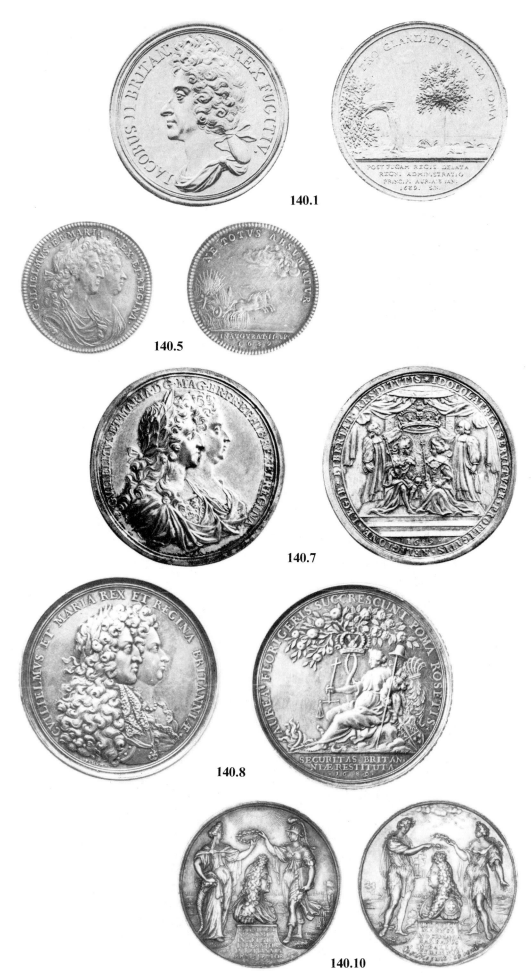

140.1

140.5

140.7

140.8

140.10

141.5

141.6

142.3

142.5

143.2

144.2

145.4

145.2

146.2

148.5

148.4

150.1

153.1

151.1

153.5

153.6

153.8

153.10

154.2

155.3

156.1

157.3

158.1

158.3
(reduced)

159.2

159.8

160.2

161.2

161.4

162.1

163.1

164.2

165.4

165.5

166.1

126

166.2

167.1

168.1

169.1

169.2

170.1

171.3

172.1

173.1

174.1

176.1

128

176.2

178.4

178.5

178.6

178.7

182.1

183.1

184.1

185.2

187.1

187.2

188.1

189.1

190.1

190.3

191.1

191.2

192.3

193.3

194.3

195.8

195.10

196.1

196.7

197.1

197.4

198.3

199.2

200.2

201.1

202.2

202.3

204.2

203.1

206.2

207.1

208.2

209.1

209.4

210.3

210.10

211.1

211.3

211.6

212.1

212.3

213.2

214.1

215.1

216.1

217.1

217.4

218.1

219.3

220.1

221.3

222.2

223.4

223.5

224.11

225.4

226.1

227.1

227.2

228.3

229.1

230.1

231.1

232.5

233.1

234.2

234.4

235.2

235.4

236.1

237.1

239.4

240.2

240.9

241.2

242.5

243.2

244.1

245.3

245.4

246.1

246.2

246.4

247.2

247.4

248.1

248.4

248.6

248.8

249.7

250.4

251.2

252.6

252.10

253.2

253.4

254.2

255.1

256.4

256.7

256.8

256.9

257.1

257.2

258.1

258.3

259.2

BATTLE OF VIMIERA
AUG XXI MDCCCVIII

259.3

WE ARE ALL BRETHREN

SLAVE TRADE ABOLISHED
BY GREAT BRITAIN
1807

THE ENGLISH ARMY ENTERS
LISBON
SEPT. MDCCCVIII

GEORGIUS.
PRINCEPS. WALLIARUM.
THEATRI.
REGIIS. INSTAURANDI. AUSPICIIS.
IN. HORTIS. BENEDICTINIS.
LONDINI.
FUNDAMENTA.
SUA. MANU. LOCAVIT
MDCCCVIII.

149

260.5

260.8

261.1

262.1

262.3

262.4

263.5

263.7

263.8

264.2

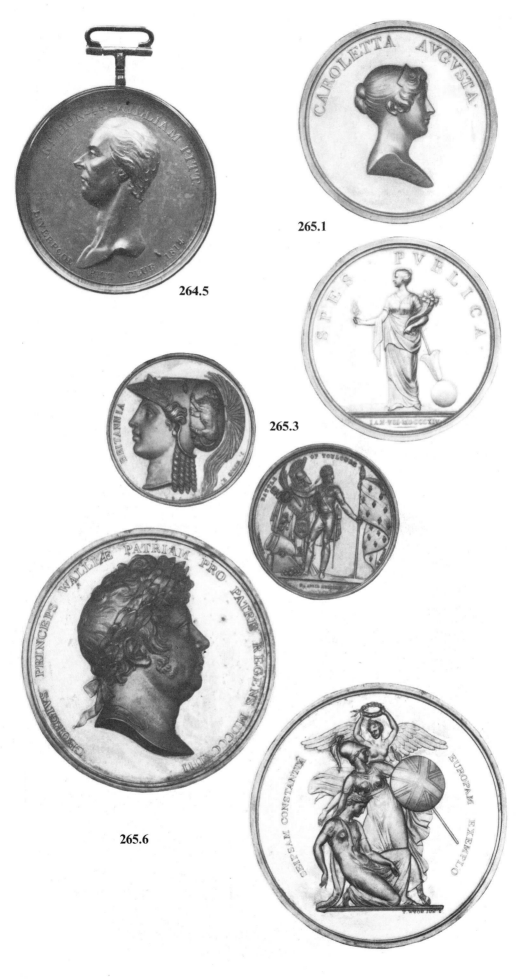

264.5

265.1

265.3

265.6

265.2

266.4

265.7

266.5

266.8

267.1

267.5

268.4

268.5

268.6

268.11

270.4

271.1

271.6

272.1

272.2

272.17

277.6

273.5

274.3

274.4

275.1

275.3

275.4

276.2

277.4

277.5

278.2

278.5

280.1

281.5

281.12

281.13

282.1

282.7

282.11

283.10

285.1

285.3

286.4

288.5

288.16

289.1

289.6

289.2

290.2

291.1

291.3

292.5

293.10

294.2

294.3

295.2

295.10

295.12

296.4

298.6

297.7

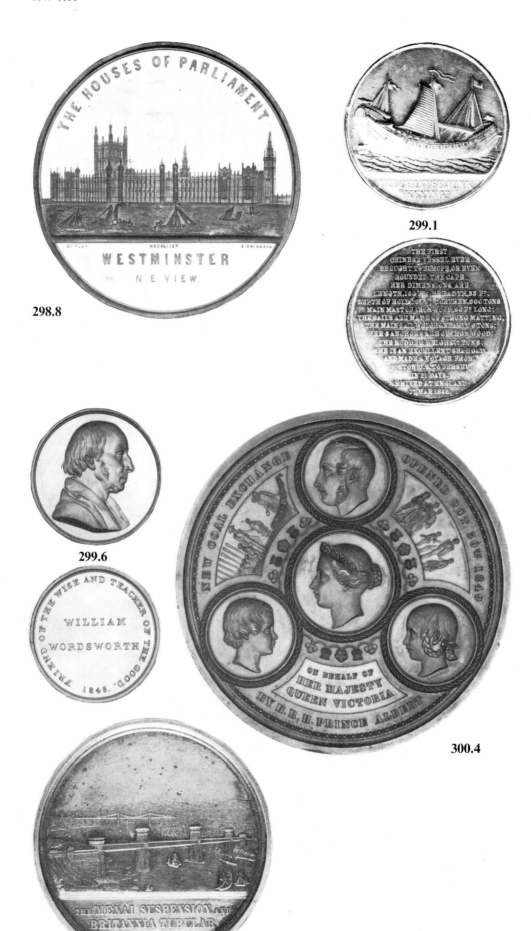

298.8

299.1

299.6

WILLIAM
WORDSWORTH

300.4

301.5

302.1

302.2

302.5

303.1

304.3

305.11

305.5

305.10

306.6

307.1

308.1

309.1

310.1

310.3

311.2

311.3

311.4

312.3

313.3

313.4

314.3

314.5

315.1

315.2

316.4

317.2

317.3

318.3

318.4

319.4

320.2

321.1

322.1

323.2

324.3

324.4

325.3

326.2

326.6

328.3

330.2

331.2

331.6

332.2

334.4

335.3

336.1

336.4

CENTENARY CELEBRATION

337.2

338.1

338.3

338.9

339.2

340.2

341.1

342.5

343.3

344.2

345.1

346.4

348.1

348.2

348.4

348.9

349.2

350.2

351.6

351.1

351.5

351.7

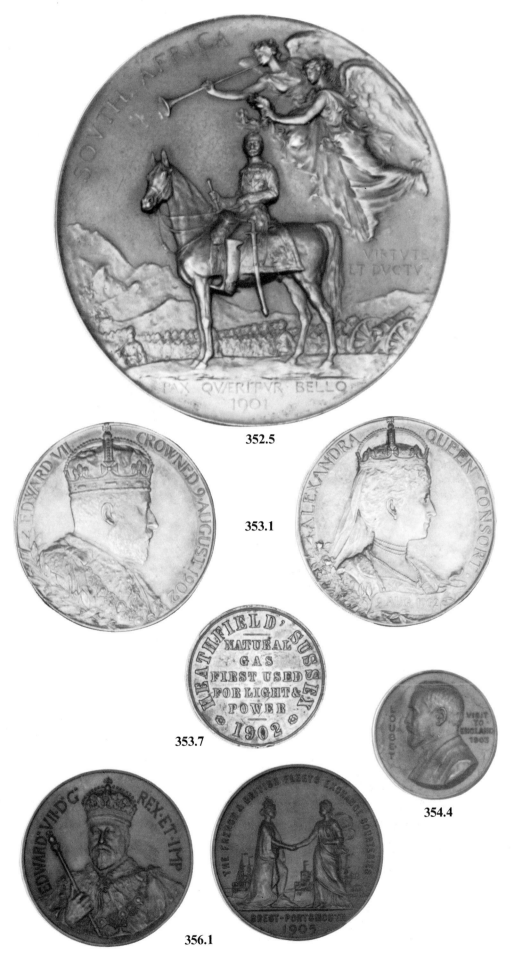

352.5

353.1

353.7

354.4

356.1

358.4

359.1

360.1

361.2

362.1

362.2

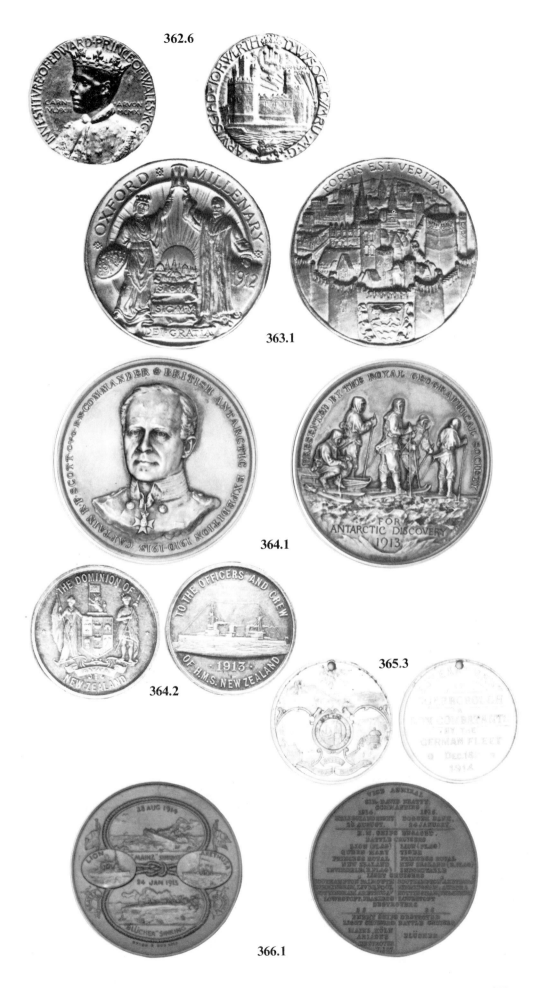

362.6

363.1

364.1

364.2

365.3

366.1

366.4

367.2

367.4

367.6

369.1

368.1

369.2

370.2

372.1

373.2

375.2

376.2

377.2

379.1

379.2

381.1

382.2

384.2

385.2

386.1

387.1

387.7

387.9

388.1

395.1

398.2

399.1

402.1

404.1

404.5

404.7

405.1

409.1

416.1

418.2

420.1

421.1

421.2

423.2

426.6

427.2

428.2

428.3

430.1

431.1

432.1

433.1

434.1

435.1

435.2

Index of Medallists

A. 231.1
Abeele, Pieter Van 111.2, 118.1
Abramson, Abraham 256.6
Adams, George Gammon
298.3, 303.1, 320.1, 328.1,
331.1, 336.3, 344.1
Adolfzoon, Christoph 118.3
Allen, Charles J. 358.2
Allen and Moore 282.11, 294.2,
294.3, 295.5, 295.8, 295.12,
296.3, 297.2, 297.4, 297.7,
298.9, 299.5, 300.2, 300.5,
301.1, 301.3, 302.1, 302.2,
302.3, 302.7, 302.8, 303.2
Andrews, D. 431.2, 431.3
Anthony, Charles 55.1
Arondeaux, Regnier 136.13,
141.5, 142.2, 148.2, 153.1
Aronson, J. 301.5
Avern, Edward 134.1, 268.5,
281.2

B. and A. 344.3
Bain, W. 273.1, 273.5, 274.4,
276.3, 281.3, 283.9, 288.11
Balfour, Sir James 101.1
Barber, J. 260.1, 265,6, 288.7,
288.17
Barker, I. 295.11
Barre, Jean Jacques 259.2,
265.11
Bayes, Gilbert 355.1, 360.2,
387.1
B. F. *see* F., B.
Birmingham Mint 325.8, 338.9,
348.4, 370.2, 404.4, 405.1,
406.1, 424.4, 425.1, 426.1,
427.1, 428.4, 430.2, 430.3
Blum, Johann 84.1
Bock, W. R. 364.2
Boehm, Sir Joseph Edgar 325.5,
326.4, 334.2, 338.1
Bonnetain, A. 366.4
Boskam, Jan 143.6, 144.2,
145.1, 145.2, 146.1, 153.7,
153.9, 154.1, 156.1
Boulton, Matthew 223.5, 240.2,
256.3
Bowcher, Frank 344.4, 345.1,
346.2, 348.2, 348.3, 348.10,
349.1, 350.1, 352.5, 353.2,
354.4, 356.4, 359.2, 359.3,
360.1, 362.2, 362.7, 364.1,
366.1, 367.2, 368.1, 370.1,
373.2, 379.1

Bower, George 113.1, 129.2,
129.3, 131.1, 132.1, 133.1,
133.2, 133.3, 134.2, 134.3,
136.6, 136.7, 136.8, 136.9,
136.10, 136.11, 138.1, 138.2,
139.1, 139.3, 139.4, 139.9,
140.3, 140.6, 140.7
Brenet, Nicolas Guy Antoine
248.8, 250.5, 250.7, 259.1,
260.6, 262.5, 263.5, 264.2,
264.4, 265.3, 266.4, 266.6,
266.9, 266.10
Briot, Nicolas 69.1, 69.2, 72.1,
73.2, 73.3, 73.4, 76.1, 76.2,
78.1, 81.2, 82.3, 86.4, 91.2
British Petroleum (issuers)
426.2
Brock, Thomas 338.8, 348.1
Brown, William 311.4
Bull, Samuel 158.2, 159.3,
160.3, 161.5
Burch, Edward 225.3, 236.2,
239.5
B., V. 387.6

Cariat, Lucien Jean Henri 361.1
Carter, J. 287.2, 290.3, 290.4,
338.5, 339.2, 339.3
Chevalier, Auguste 326.2
Chevalier, Nicolas 128.1
Clint, Scipio 279.3, 281.14
Coincraft 423.4
Colley, L. G. 419.1
Collis, G. R. 288.1, 288.14,
289.5
Couriguer, Joseph Anton 260.5
Crichton, J. 346.4
Croker, John 148.4, 153.3,
153.4, 153.5, 153.6, 153.8,
153.10, 154.2, 155.1, 155.2,
155.4, 157.1, 157.2, 158.1,
158.2, 158.3, 159.3, 159.5,
159.6, 159.8, 160.1, 160.2,
160.3, 161.2, 161.3, 161.4,
161.5, 162.1, 164.1, 164.2,
165.3, 165.4, 165.5, 166.1,
166.2, 168.1, 169.1, 169.3,
169.5, 176.1, 178.2, 178.6,
178.7, 182.1, 183.1
Cropanese, Filippo 217.3

Dadler, Sebastian 84.2
Danbury Mint 426.3

Darby, A. C. 325.3
Dassier, Jacques Antoine 191.2,
192.4, 193.2, 194.4, 194.6,
195.2, 195.3, 195.4, 195.5,
195.6, 195.7, 195.8, 195.9,
202.3
Dassier, Jean 125.2, 145.3,
155.5, 169.4, 173.1, 176.2,
178.3, 178.4, 178.5, 180.1,
180.2, 182.2, 182.3, 211.3
Davies, J. 240.1, 240.5
Davis, Joseph 283.3, 283.5,
284.3, 285.1, 286.3, 288.3,
288.5, 289.3, 289.6, 291.8,
292.3, 293.1, 293.3, 293.6,
293.7, 293.8, 293.10, 294.4,
294.6, 295.4, 295.7, 295.9,
295.10, 297.3, 298.1, 298.10
Demanet, V. 389.2
Depaulis, Alexis Joseph 266.3,
266.4, 266.8, 268.1, 268.10
Desboeufs, Antoine 271.10
Dicks, D. 367.8
Dixon, Roger 240.6
Doman, Charles Leighfield
369.2, 382.1
Domard, Joseph François 301.4
Dowler, G. 311.2
Drappentier, D. 164.3
Dressler, Conrad 331.2, 332.5
Dropsy, Henry 404.2
Droz, Jean-Pierre 240.2, 246.1,
255.4, 264.4
Dubois, Etienne Jacques 260.6,
262.4
Dulac, Edmund 413.1
Dumarest, Rambert 249.9
Dupré, Augustin 230.3
Durand, Amédée 107.1
Durbin, Leslie 428.2, 431.1
Dutton, Ron 433.4
Du Vivier, Pierre Simon
Benjamin 227.2, 232.3

Elderton, Robert 426.4
Elkan, Benno 389.4
Elkington & Co. 337.1, 337.4,
342.1, 353.4
Ellis, R. 275.5

F. 92.8
F., B. 223.5
Fattorini Bros. 361.5, 385.3,
404.6